CAT 5

CAT 5

R. D. DILDAY

Published by Storm Publishing
Seattle, WA

Author's Note

Numerous agencies and experts provided information for this book. A modicum of literary license was taken in the writing of this book to sustain the appropriate dramatic tone.

This book is a work of fiction. The characters, events and places in this book are either fictional or used fictitiously. Any similarity between the characters in this book and any person, living or dead, is entirely coincidental.

CAT 5

Copyright 2004 by R.D. Dilday

Cover image provided by NASA Goddard Laboratory for Atmospheres, data from NOAA. Cover design by Jeanette Alexander.

Published by Storm Publishing
Seattle
Please visit us on the web:
www.stormpublishing.com

ISBN: 0-9748905-1-0 Softcover Edition
Library of Congress Catalog Card Number: 2004091078

First edition: July 2004

Printed in the United States of America

DEDICATION

This book is lovingly dedicated to my wife, Dorrie, and the kids—for encouraging me to set off in the first place and keeping the wind in my sails.

ACKNOWLEDGMENTS

Special thanks to the staff at the National Hurricane Center, for tirelessly answering my questions and showing me around the place. Thanks, also, to the men and women of NOAA.

Special thanks to the 53rd Weather Reconnaissance Squadron and Captain Scott Dommin, U.S. Air Force (retired) for helping with the technical aspects of hurricane hunting and aviation.

I would also like to thank my good friend, Charles Hegelheimer, a man who knows a great deal about airplanes.

Thanks also go to Robin Smith, for her sharp editorial eye.

As much as it is possible to do so in a work of fiction, I have tried to remain true to the facts and details. Technical errors and omissions are mine alone and were committed in the name of dramatic expression or for purely stylistic reasons.

When the wind is still, the trees cease to dance.

PROLOGUE

Dome Exploration's Deepwater II
The Bay of Bengal

Professor Yoshida watched a pencil roll across the conference table and felt the sway of the sea. The door creaked open and several men filed into the cramped meeting room.

The head of engineering was the last one inside, and he dogged the steel door before removing his hard hat. "I think we all know each other," he said, turning to face Sanford Polk, Dome's chairman and CEO.

Yoshida bowed, then sat.

"Let's get on with it," Polk boomed.

The engineer cleared his throat. "Seems there have been rumblings of safety violations associated with our recent oil drilling activities."

"Horseshit!" Polk said, motioning toward a window overlooking the drilling platform. "If it's so dangerous, why do we have fifty applicants for every job on this rig?"

The room went silent.

The engineer addressed Yoshida. "Besides the safety violations, we've also been accused of drilling in ecologically sensitive waters that are prone to severe storms."

Yoshida knew what they wanted to hear. If the company could curry a favorable opinion on the subject of the storm threat, drilling would likely continue uninterrupted.

"Hell, back in the Gulf, we rode it out with the worst of them," Polk added. "These jack towers can be raised and lowered to meet all known sea conditions."

The Japanese meteorologist studied a cluster of instruments and let his eyes linger on the falling barometer. Outside, an anemometer spun like a top. Polk may have had an unwavering faith in the structure's integrity, but it was an opinion Yoshida didn't share.

A pilot burst through the door. "If you plan to get off this rig by air, you'd better continue this meeting aboard the helicopter. The Joint Typhoon Warning Center's predicting something big."

Unable to remain silent, Yoshida said, "Perhaps you should concentrate on getting your crew safely ashore."

The comment was met with dull stares—and, one by one, the men donned their hard hats and stepped outside into the weather.

Beneath the converging clouds, roughnecks in orange slickers scrambled about the platform. Yoshida clung to a wet steel railing and faced the oncoming front. Perhaps his old friend Samuelson was right.

He heard the unmistakable whine of turbines and watched the rotor begin to turn. The engineer called from the Bell 427's open door, beckoning him aboard.

A few moments later, the drilling platform disappeared in the distance.

"So, what's the verdict?" Polk asked.

Yoshida studied him over the top of his glasses. "I think you need a bigger rig."

CHAPTER 1

Carolina bound

A late model pickup barreled north on I-95, just past Hardeeville and the South Carolina state line. Several tarp-covered boxes filled the truck bed.

Jon Samuelson, the driver, glanced through a pair of wire-rims into the rearview mirror and motioned over his shoulder with his thumb. "That's it, the last of my worldly belongings."

Erik Reynard, the younger of the two, sat shotgun and nodded. He fidgeted with the radio until the stray notes of an accordion crackled between a John Deere commercial and an evangelist preaching about the end of the world. "There's something to be said for a minimalist lifestyle, no entanglements."

"Got a point there," Samuelson said, staring out at the horizon. "Hard to believe the drought's still punishing the Midwest. You'd never guess by the looks of those clouds."

"Sshh!" said Erik. "I know this song."

"You and your swamp pop."

"The word's zydeco," Erik said. "Lord, what I'd give for a cell phone that worked out here."

"Even if you were the first caller, what in the world would you do with a case of Cajun seasoning?"

"Give it to you, let you whip up some of those blackened sea bass fillets you're so famous for."

"Never know, we might just get in some fishing before you have to head back to Miami. Hurricane season doesn't officially

3

start for a couple days yet. How's the new director working out?"

Erik spit an empty sunflower shell out the window. "Let's just say you're sorely missed."

"If I'd known NOAA was going to be spun off by the Department of Commerce, I might have done things differently."

"Wasn't your fault," Erik said. "Say, how 'bout I join you on the island?"

"You'd be wasting your talents out there, digging around in the silt and mud. Doesn't pay much, either—fifty percent of nothing is nothing."

"You don't seem to mind."

"I don't need much to get by," said Samuelson. "Some mullet for bait, a pound of coffee now and then, and a little grant money to pay the coring contractor."

"I don't need much, either," Erik said, getting his chin up.

"What you have is a nose for storms. It's a God-given thing and it's best to use it."

Erik studied Samuelson's face, tanned and wrinkled. "Why do I get the impression you'd say anything to discourage me from leaving the Hurricane Center?"

"Because it's in your best interest to stay there. If it hadn't been for my run-in with the Weather Czar, I'd probably still be there myself."

Erik turned his gaze out the side window. "Never know, I might be an asset."

"You've got more important things to do, protecting people and property."

Discouraged, Erik snapped a rubber band around a bag of sunflower seeds and worked it into his pack. Most of his friends back home were using the Memorial Day holiday as an excuse to head for the beach. Not him. Nobody special was waiting in the wings, just an old friend needing a hand.

He raised the binoculars and stared at a far-off curtain of rain. "Hell of a microburst moving ashore. Look there, you can even see the toes."

"If you really want to do me a favor, you'll keep an eye on the Atlantic Conveyor—let me know when the big one's coming."

"Nothing gets past NEXRAD," Erik boasted. "Our Doppler's state of the art, remember?"

"It's not the radar I'm talking about."

Erik lowered the binoculars and watched the interstate snake by. "Come to think of it, you've been pretty quiet about your research lately. You're on to something, I can feel it."

Samuelson flipped the wipers to high and stared into the rain without saying a word. Slowly, he reached into his coat pocket and withdrew a pale white rock.

"Check this out," he said, tossing the specimen to Erik.

"What is it?"

"A window into the past, ancient coral from a reef terrace in New Guinea. My theory's coming together like a Swiss watch."

"More global warming?" Erik said. "Come on, this isn't the tabloids. Give me something I can use back in forecasting."

"It's all there in the geological record, laid down like dinosaur bones."

Erik tossed the coral in his hand. "Footprints in the sand, Jon. This sample tells us where we've been, that's all."

"Perhaps, or maybe we're entering a rare weather cycle seen once every thousand millennia."

"You've been out in the islands too long."

Back in the truck bed, a tarp suddenly tore loose and flapped about wildly.

"My journals!" Samuelson yelled, pulling to the shoulder. "My whole life's wrapped up in those boxes."

As soon as the pickup ground to a stop, the doors flew open. The wind picked up, and the sky crackled with lightning.

Samuelson leaned inside the truck bed and tossed a tie-down rope to Erik. "I'm dead serious about the weather," he said. "It's changing."

"Suppose it is, what do you expect me to do about it?"

"Just keep an eye out."

CHAPTER 2

The National Hurricane Center
Florida International University

An oppressive cloud layer settled over south Florida during the first week of hurricane season like a lid on a pot of steamed clams. Inside the center, Dr. Erik Reynard hunched over a computer monitor, studying the deteriorating weather with considerable interest before giving his mouse a click.

"Gotcha," he said, watching the storm's position print out on the neighboring RAMDIS satellite display.

Arlene's counterclockwise rotation began fifteen-hundred miles southeast of Miami in an area of the Atlantic known as the Lesser Antilles, a notoriously prolific spawning ground for tropical storms, and, on occasion, hurricanes. Erik had been the first to spot the disturbance, even won a ten-dollar wager when she became a named storm.

A freckled technician craned his neck around the doorway. "Deevers is looking for you. Here's some light reading courtesy of Forecasting Support, catch."

Erik caught the airborne folder and parked it on the corner of his desk.

"Better watch it," the tech added. "He's on the warpath this morning."

Erik turned his attention back to the dubious formation on his satellite display. He figured it would be a long shift; the storm appeared to be deepening.

6

Inside the folder he found a neatly folded newspaper and several weather reports. One look at the super typhoon dominating the front page and he realized Asia was having its problems, too. He'd received a preliminary glimpse of the storm a week earlier, care of a friend over at the Department of Defense. Early satellite reconnaissance of the area looked pretty grim.

The Joint Typhoon Warning Center in Hawaii had picked up the storm first, said it looked like a real sonofabitch, a potential monster, easily Category 4 territory. Erik knew the damage would be considerable—the A.P. wire photos really brought the level of destruction home.

Standing, he tossed the newspaper atop a six-foot pile threatening to engulf his office and gulped the last slug of coffee from a chipped mug bearing the inscription Camille. He snatched a picture from an overflowing bookshelf—better times, he and Samuelson fishing along the South Carolina coast.

His friend was on to something all right, insisting the answer to the climatic puzzle wouldn't be found in the skies, but under their feet in the geological record. "You want to understand the weather?" he was fond of saying. "Then dig."

If nothing else, Samuelson was committed to what he believed. After losing the directorship at the Hurricane Center, he began searching for weather clues in the prehistoric silt and pollen he collected from the Florida Keys north to the Outer Banks.

Erik hadn't been able to reach his friend for days, and he was more than a little anxious to confirm their rendezvous later that month. Glancing at his reflection in the window, he tucked his shoulder-length hair down the collar of his shirt. He'd catch up with the paleoclimatologist soon enough, but first he had a damn press conference to give.

The sound of heavy footsteps plodded down the hall. A few moments later Deevers appeared, a fifty-nine-year-old bulldog with small steely eyes better suited for audits than weather analysis, pinpoints staring from a ball of soft dough.

The director glanced disapprovingly at the stack of newspapers. "We've got trash cans around here, you know."

"That's not trash," Erik said. "It's paper, perfectly recyclable cellulose."

"I've got a media room crawling with reporters, what the

hell are you waiting for?"

"More dead trees," Erik said, lifting the reports from his desk.

Deevers polished a can of soda, played a little waste can basketball, then reached inside his coat for an envelope. "You're heading for Houston first thing tomorrow. You'll find tickets and an itinerary inside."

"What about Arlene?"

Deevers feigned a frown. "Guess we'll have to manage without you."

Erik pinned the envelope to his desk with a small stone archer he'd picked up on a scientific exchange to China's notorious Black Dragon River.

There was no sense debating his upcoming travel plans. Come morning, he'd be on his way to Texas. He bent down to retrieve the empty soda can from the trash and brushed past Deevers on his way to the Environmental Lab. What the hell, a few days away from the center might just do him some good.

After rounding the corner, he wove through the Tropical Prediction Center, studying the reports along the way. An intern trotted down a converging hall, clutching a stack of files against her chest. Tai Jeffers was the last person Samuelson had hired before his unexpected departure, a doctoral candidate out of U.C. Davis.

"Wait up," she said, tugging at Erik's elbow.

"I hate press conferences."

"You'll need these files," she said, matching his stride. "It's the latest on the storm. By the way, the report's in on that airline crash in Phoenix, evening news reported it was due to clear air turbulence."

"How do they know that? The FAA team just touched down."

Tai shrugged. "That's what some local meteorologist reported."

"Rank amateurs, the entire lot."

"Perhaps, but they're making three times what we are. Just think, all you'd have to do is put on a coat and tie and wear a carnation in your lapel. Come on, don't tell me you've never fantasized about reporting the weather for one of the networks.

Anyway, here's your chance to dazzle them," she said, sliding a second report under his arm, "ingested satellite data just in from NESDIS."

"What would I do without you?"

"Fail horribly," she said with a smile, "and don't forget it."

He slipped inside the Media Room and reached the news desk a few seconds later.

A reporter rose from a folding chair. "Has the tropical depression been upgraded or not?"

Erik lifted a pointer and picked his words wisely. Meeting the press was like talking to children, always the risk of being misquoted. The last thing he wanted to do was create a panic. Premature evacuations were costly and easily ran into the millions. Still, he remembered Samuelson's warning and figured it was best to be cautious. After all, people's lives were potentially at stake.

He aimed his pointer at a screen depicting the Caribbean, stopping several inches east of St. Lucia Island where a whirling mass of clouds began to take on the characteristic signature of a major storm system.

"This," he said, looking slowly around the room, "is Arlene. We've just upgraded her to a tropical storm, and we'll be monitoring her closely."

A woman in the front row shot up her right hand, her fingers long and well-manicured. A mane of blonde curls cascaded down the front of her silk blouse, and the fingers of her other hand were busy counting the pearls of her necklace.

Erik squinted to make out her press badge through the blaze of camera lights and thought it said Heather. She looked somewhat out of place, better suited to report on South Florida's trendy cafes.

"Was the storm triggered by El Nino?" she asked. "And what about the drought?"

Snickers and groans rippled through the sea of hardened storm reporters. It was clear from her question she was new to the weather beat.

Deciding not to shoot her down in flames, Erik leaned forward with an explanation. "The last El Nino officially ended four years ago. We're now experiencing a phenomenon called La Nina, sometimes referred to as El Viejo. You know, the ENSO cycle?

The southern oscillation?"

It was clear from the reporter's blank stare that she didn't know. Erik spotted Tai off to the side of the room. She'd caught him admiring the reporter's long legs.

Privately, he feared the upcoming storm season might pack some nasty surprises, a somber opinion shared by nearly every other specialist and forecaster at the Hurricane Center. Conditions were indeed ripe. High altitude equatorial winds had shifted in a westerly direction, and West African rainfall was well above normal. Meanwhile, the Caribbean was experiencing unusually high temperatures.

Erik surveyed the sea of weather professionals seated before him and realized there was no need in stating the obvious. Every journalist in the room knew it was shaping up to be one hell of a storm season, save for the lovely Ms. El Nino seated in the front row. She had unwittingly conjured up the one atmospheric event capable of improving an overly active hurricane season. The devastating rain and overheated Pacific aside, El Nino-driven winds had the desirable tendency of leveling Atlantic hurricanes like bowling pins.

Just then, Deevers entered the rear of the Media Room. Perhaps it was time to test the waters with Samuelson's controversial weather theory. Erik hesitated for a moment before dropping his bombshell.

"A new body of research points to a marked increase in violent storms," he said.

The room buzzed with interest, and Deevers' face went crimson. He made a slicing motion across his throat with his hand and stormed the news desk. "What Dr. Reynard is trying to say is that we'll continue to monitor the Atlantic for signs of severe storms, and we'll be watching Arlene closely."

A dozen hands shot up.

"At present, the storm poses no threat to life or property," Deevers went on. "If the present situation deteriorates, the press will be notified immediately."

He turned his back to the audience, brushed past Erik and whispered, "Pull that again and it's your ass."

Erik watched him blast through the exit door and decided it was best to scale back his rhetoric. After all, the storm remained well offshore. A proper evacuation could easily be called in the unlikely event it became necessary to do so.

He stuck around to field several closing questions. With the drought well into its fourth devastating year, the weather was on everyone's mind. He discounted exaggerated suggestions of global weather changes despite the Midwest's crippling drought, tornadoes near Los Angeles and the freakish snowfalls blanketing the deserts of the southwest.

But what if the weather really was changing? He seemed to hear it everywhere, from the swing-shift manager at the corner bookstore to the old Cuban woman at the neighborhood dry cleaners, even the mechanic at the garage where he serviced his trusty Saab.

He recalled Samuelson's assertion, that current climatic changes were the harbingers of phenomenal weather cycles—an interesting theory, if nothing else.

Heather lingered until most of the other reporters had gone. She possessed the sort of stunning good looks he'd admired among Tulane's least attainable coeds—the belles lined up outside Le Bon Temp, The Boot and Igor's.

"Thanks for going easy on me back there," she said, flipping her hair over her shoulder. "I'm new to the weather desk."

"It was a legitimate question," he said, squaring his reports into a pile. "About El Nino, I mean."

"I felt like such an idiot. Anyway, this weather gig's temporary."

"Gig?"

"Six years of college with a masters in journalism—you don't think I'm here by choice, do you?"

Transfixed, Erik remained silent.

"Anyway, I'm supposed to be covering national news," she said with a shrug. "Beats working the classifieds."

"I'm sure it does."

The weather meant everything to Erik—it was his world. He managed an awkward smile and wanted to say something flattering, something clever, maybe make small talk and ask what she was doing for the rest of his life, but no.

"You see," he said, interlocking his fingers, "the southern oscillation works like this, it's sort of an atmospheric tug of war between the eastern and western hemispheres, between sea level pressure differences and oceanic temperature anomalies."

A glaze formed over her eyes like she'd been flash frozen.

"R-r-right," she said.

"The weather affects everything, from world financial markets to fishing and agriculture, even the spread of disease and the migration of insects."

"Interesting," she said, looking like she meant it.

He watched the wheels turn behind her baby blues as she switched on a fetching smile and offered her hand. "My name's Heather Conroy."

"Erik," he said, feeling as though he'd blown his chances, like she cared about the southern oscillation for Christ's sake.

Nothing clever came to mind, and he just stood there, sporting a dumb grin.

"I should be going," she said. "Thanks for the explanation."

She caught up with her photographer and disappeared beneath an illuminated exit sign.

The lights dimmed, microphones were withdrawn and Erik ambled back up the hall, wishing he knew half as much about women as he did about the weather.

As he rounded the corner and headed for his office, Deevers emerged from the shadows. "Nice little stunt back there."

"Ever stop to think Samuelson might be onto something? If he is, people have a right to know."

"Your job's to forecast storms, unless you want to end up like your friend."

"What happened to Samuelson was pathetic."

Deevers glanced up at a portrait of the newly appointed Secretary of Weather and said, "Maybe he shouldn't have bucked the Weather Czar."

"Bobby Ocean? He's a hack."

"He's also chairman of Ocean Broadcasting, Secretary of the Department of Weather and your boss. You'd do well to remember that."

"Anything else?"

"Come morning, just make sure you're on that plane."

CHAPTER 3

Mr. Weatherman

Tai swung into Erik's office with an armful of reports. "Gee, Mr. Weatherman, what makes the wind blow?"

"Very funny."

"I see your pupil stayed around for a little private tutoring."

"It's her first major storm, okay?" He felt himself blush and sniffed the air. "New perfume?"

"Sirocco," the black forecaster said. "Didn't think you'd notice."

"Seems somehow appropriate. You know, Sirocco...the wind? Question is, does the Colonel like it?"

"Who do you think bought it for me?"

She moved toward the room's concrete wall as if drawn to the tick of rain against the small window there, its inch-and-a-half thick pane a laminate of high-impact acrylic and glass.

"It's beginning to rain," she said, letting her fingertip circle around inside the fogged panel, making a smiley face. "I'm told these windows can stop airborne bricks."

Erik rose and stared past her. "Think I'd put my money on the brick."

Backing slowly from the glass, he watched the rain dapple his view of the street beyond and caught a glimpse of his past in the distorted pane. He recalled the night the levee broke and felt a shiver.

"You look a million miles away," she said.

"It's nothing. Just sometimes I feel like we're missing something, despite all this technology."

"Sounds like you've been talking to Samuelson again."

He turned from the window. "I'm meeting him on Pritchard's Island, later this month."

"You sure got Deevers' attention with that severe weather stuff."

"Sonofabitch had it coming. He's sending me to Houston first thing tomorrow."

"I guess that means our run is out."

"Afraid so."

Tai thumbed through a report. "You might want to have a look at this, your storm crossed fifty-five degrees."

Erik looked up.

"That's not all. There's a cruise ship out there, reporting sixty knot gusts and thirty-foot seas."

Erik pulled on his glasses for a better look. "They're heading straight into the storm. Aren't they receiving a satellite feed?"

Tai shrugged.

"What do we know about the ship?"

"Name's La Reina Del Mar, two-hundred-sixty-two meters, Panamanian registry, sixty-eight thousand tons—says here she cruises at twenty-four knots."

"Fast ship," he said. "She'll need it. What's her capacity?"

Her eyes rose slowly from the ship's manifest. "Two-thousand-thirty-two."

"Are you telling me there are two thousand people sailing into that storm?"

"Over twenty-nine hundred, including the crew."

He reckoned the ship's precise location and wondered how many other vessels might be in the area.

"If that storm keeps spinning up, she could reach hurricane force—better get this update over to the Coast Guard. Tell them to get that cruise ship the hell out of there. Has the 53rd out of Keesler been notified?"

"A WC-130 will be airborne within ninety minutes."

"How do you know that?"

"The Colonel just called to cancel our date, looks like he won't be out till the weekend."

CHAPTER 4

Keesler Air Force Base
Biloxi, Mississippi

Michael Simms steered toward the guard gate while the air conditioning in his Firebird struggled to keep up with the soaring humidity. Nearby, a group of kids struggled to get a kite off the ground. Above them, gulls sailed across the mackerel sky.

A vague feeling of unease prickled up his spine, the same apprehension he'd experienced flying sorties out of Turkey's Incirlik Air Base. But this wasn't Iraq or the Balkans. No flak would be flying, and there would be no missiles to dodge, no counter-measures to deploy and nowhere to hide. This time the enemy was nature whose frenzied forces had once more run amok.

No two reconnaissance missions were exactly alike, and Michael learned early there was no such thing as a routine flight. He listened to the mellow vibes piping through his stereo and began to chill. The weekend was just around the corner—providing all hell didn't break loose, he'd have Tai to himself for two days straight.

Slowing to a stop beside the guard shack, he lowered his window and felt a wave of heat against his face. He breathed the syrupy Mississippi air and felt it settle in his lungs.

A beefy young guard slouched beside the gate, hair black and fuzz short. Sweat dampened wide patches beneath his arms. The moment he spotted the silver oak leaves on Michael's shoulder, he snapped to attention and offered a stiff salute.

"At ease," Michael said, pulling at his collar. "It's hotter than a ripe habanero."

"Yessir," said the guard.

Michael idled beneath the rising gate. The sight of the Air Force brats reminded him of his youth, of summer days spent dreaming of piloting a bird of his own. He glanced through the upper half of the windshield at a wind sock flapping near the tower.

Up ahead, several specially equipped, WC-130 Hercules waited on the tarmac. He parked and reached into the back seat to retrieve a brochure advertising engagement rings. After slipping it into his briefcase, he eased his tall frame from the car.

Nearby, an elderly Asian man opened the trunk of a Chevy sedan and removed an overnight bag. Appearing disoriented, he paused to consult a note he pulled from his shirt pocket. His forehead bore the liver spots of age, and his posture was hunched as if his slight frame had given in to the gravity of his years.

Michael closed the distance between them. "Can I help you?"

The man refolded the note and tamped sweat from his forehead with a handkerchief. "I'm looking for the Hurricane Hunters, the 53rd Weather Recon Squadron."

"You've come to the right place, I'll show you the way."

Michael led the visitor toward a room where a group of Air Force personnel were assembled. His commanding officer, Red York called him to the edge of the room.

The 53rd Weather Reconnaissance Squadron was York's baby. He'd been with the elite unit since the early days, flying recon out of Hunter AFB.

Meanwhile, the elderly visitor paused to study a wall crowded with weather photos.

"Know who that is?" York whispered, nodding in the direction of the visitor.

Michael shrugged. "He followed me in, said he was looking for the Hurricane Hunters."

"Name's Yoshida," York said. "Teaches weather over at Texas Tech."

"Professor Yoshida?" Michael said. "I'm impressed."

"You've heard of him?"

"He's pretty well known in weather circles. Tai raved about a paper he'd written for the Intergovernmental Panel on Climate Change."

"Jap bastard's more infamous than famous," York whispered, leveling his stare on the elder scientist.

Michael stiffened at the word Jap. He'd never seen York's racist stripes before, and the slur stopped him cold. He'd never figured York for a bigot.

"What do you mean, infamous?"

"He got his start at the Central Meteorological Bureau in Tokyo, before the war. Left the Bureau to help the military launch more than nine thousand fugos, weather balloons rigged with incendiary bombs. They launched the damn things towards the U.S., sailed them into the jet stream."

"They do any damage?"

"Not much. Less than three hundred ever touched down. They killed a few civilians and set some forest fires. The government kept a lid on their existence until after the war. Sort of ironic, though."

"How so?" Michael asked.

"One fugo actually shut down a plutonium breeding reactor near Cold Creek. After the war, it was rumored the Japanese had considered equipping them with biological and chemical weapons. Who knows? Anyway, I may have to accommodate the son of a bitch to keep our friends over at NOAA happy, but he's not flying with me. We've got two birds going up, and he flies with you."

"Yes, sir."

York studied Michael for a moment as if waiting for a protest, but none came. "Good, it's settled then."

Michael tried to understand York's prejudice, having little tolerance for that sort of thing himself. His grandfather used to tell him about the old days, tough times in the delta, plowing worn-out hardpan with a pickax to afford an occasional tin of coffee in town. But bigotry and hatred can only keep you down so long, and the Simms family finally got its wings. The Air Force had been good to him.

Michael called Yoshida to the middle of the room where a half-dozen officers had gathered. The meteorologist disappeared in the huddle of flight-suited reservists. He looked small to be so notorious.

"Listen up. This is Dr. Yoshida—he's on loan to NOAA from Texas Tech where he's a tenured professor of atmospheric science. Give him your full cooperation. This is his first flight with the Hurricane Hunters, and I want it to be a memorable trip."

After the briefing, Michael introduced Yoshida individually to each member of the crew. To his copilot, Lt. Colonel Martini he whispered, "Make sure he's got a burp bag in his lap before we get off the ground."

The crew-members hit the tarmac and moved out toward a pair of Lockheed WC-130's waiting on the flight line. Michael slowed to accompany the professor while his crew moved out ahead.

"My girlfriend's a big fan of yours."

"Was she a student of mine?"

"No, she's with the National Hurricane Center," he said, slowing to a stop. "Mind if I ask you a question?"

"What is it?"

"No disrespect meant, but I heard you were involved in Japan's fugo project during the war." Michael paused for a few long seconds and broke off eye contact. The question begged an answer, and he dug the heel of his boot into a crack in the runway.

"The past is sometimes best left in the past, Colonel."

"Sorry, I didn't mean to get personal."

"You have nothing to be sorry for. Truth is, I did work on the project. When the war turned against Imperial Japan, it was believed the same divine wind that had delivered our island-nation from Kubla Khan could somehow be evoked to help us prevail over the United States. But that was not to be." Yoshida moved toward the plane. "After all, we were unable to stop the bomb."

The statement bristled with a strange, all but forgotten nationalism.

"But you're a scientist," Michael protested. "Why'd you take part in a weapons' project?"

"Individual rights didn't matter much in 1944. Objecting to Imperial policy meant death or incarceration, and I had a wife and young son to care for."

Thinking it best to change the subject, Michael said, "Do

you and your family live in Lubbock?"

Yoshida inched toward the plane's open door and turned to face him. "My wife and infant son lived in Hiroshima."

CHAPTER 5

Altitude: 14,950 feet
The West Indies

The big bird thundered toward its rendezvous with Arlene. Yoshida had taken up position near the aerial reconnaissance weather officer to observe the collection of storm data firsthand.

Several hours had passed since they left Keesler, and Michael still felt like he'd been kicked in the gut. Perhaps Yoshida was right, maybe the past was best left in the past. He'd lost his entire family for God's sake.

Craning his neck to see, Michael stared past the engineer and navigator to where the old man sat—erect, motionless, hands folded peaceably in his lap.

He turned back around and gazed through the windshield, unable to get the image of Yoshida's wife and child out of his head.

"What's up?" his copilot asked. "You haven't said squat since we left Keesler."

Michael looked over at Martini, then rolled a glance out the port window to study a wall of thunder clouds off in the distance.

"Got a lot on my mind," he boomed, in order to be heard over the roar of the turboprops. He felt the sixteen-thousand horsepower throb through the controls and figured it would be showtime in less than an hour. "How about some coffee before we punch through this baby?"

"No sweat," Martini said, unbuckling his harness. "How

do you want it?"

"Black with sugar." He hesitated for a moment and said, "Martini?"

"Yes, sir."

"Make sure our passenger's got his bag stowed."

As the copilot wormed his way aft, Michael stared down at a laminated picture of Tai he'd clipped to his flight plan. Standing behind her were two older women, his mother and Aunt Ida. He kissed his finger and tapped it against the photograph for luck.

Thirty-six and still a bachelor. Marrying Tai would give his mother and auntie something to celebrate—after all, they both adored her. His auntie had no children of her own, never even married. Treated Michael like she'd birthed him herself. The way his mother told it, she'd stayed at her bedside throughout the long labor.

After his father died in a pipeline explosion, his aunt took the small bedroom off the kitchen—helped his mother around the house and worked part-time at the local library. On Sundays, she played the organ at Delta Methodist Church. This may have been somewhat by design as it got her close to Reverend James whom she referred to as a little bit of heaven dressed up like a man. But he was properly married, and she a God-fearing woman, "and that," she used to say, "was that."

Michael had too many eyes on him as a boy ever to stray very far. Looking back on his childhood, he was grateful. Tai liked to tease him about all the female attention, worrying aloud that there might not be enough room in his life for another woman.

When he teased her back about the tough competition, she took a swing at him and landed both of them flat on their backs in a field of wildflowers. He didn't discover until much later that the ladies in his life had been in cahoots all along. He'd be marrying Tai Jeffers—that had been ordained.

Michael wondered about what he would do if he left the Air Force Reserve for a more routine job. He could always fly for one of the airlines, but hiring among the commercial carriers was cyclical. Job security had been one of his key considerations in joining the Air Force, but who would have speculated an end to the cold war? Still, the world was far from safe—September 11th had changed all that forever.

As dire as the weather had become, the job wasn't without certain fringe benefits. No one dared tamper with budgets scheduled to sustain the elite weather unit, not with the current drought.

The Hercules banked in a graceful arc, sunlight flashing from its wings. Off in the distance, a thunderhead rose like a billowing chimney. It resembled the characteristic mushroom cloud of a nuclear bomb blast, of the detonated *Little Boy* over Hiroshima, perhaps.

For an instant, Michael contemplated leaving the controls unattended and moving aft, to tell Yoshida how sorry he was, to apologize for his family being vaporized, to turn back the hands of time and bring them back, to explain it was during a time of war and somehow forgivable. But, ultimately, cool military instincts took over, and his conscience was quieted. He remained at the controls and took a deep meditative breath.

"Here you go," Martini said, handing off a steaming cup of java before climbing back in his seat.

Seated behind them was the flight engineer. Behind him sat the navigator who was busy receiving data from CARCAH, the Center's Chief Aerial Reconnaissance Coordination, All Hurricanes.

"Buckle up, Buttercups," Michael announced through his mike. "And make sure all loose gear is stowed. We'll be making our first pass at 10,000 feet."

The nose dipped, and the plane began its descent. Michael leveled off and aimed the Hercules at the heart of the huge atmospheric whirlpool.

At the rear of the aircraft, the weather officer jotted something into his log. Information collection had begun, but something was wrong. The Hurricane Center's garbled radio transmission complained about a break in their data link.

"What's the matter?" Michael said, reading exasperation in the weather officer's voice.

"Beats me," he said, banging his palm against a bank of radios. "Our satellite link's fritzing out, I'm getting some heavy duty interference here."

"Well, fix it!" Michael said. "This is no exercise."

"Roger," said the weather officer.

The storm loomed, massive and foreboding. Rain drilled the windshield as they punched their way through bands of feeder clouds. Following his navigator's directive, Michael felt his way slowly through the storm.

A sudden flash of lightning was followed almost immediately by the bump of a thunder clap. Rays of sunlight flashed through the cockpit as the plane passed in and out of the clouds, then came an unmistakable shaking.

The wings shuddered, and Michael tightened his grip on the yoke. He made mental small talk, pondering the riveter who had attached the plane's wings, hoping he'd had a good day when the Hercules he was flying came down the line.

Momentarily closing his eyes, Michael tried to erase the thought of riveter as gremlin. After all, *a pound of paper for a pound of part* had nearly become a mantra at the Pentagon, pretty much guaranteeing that someone, somewhere, had signed off on the integrity of the wings.

The plane's huge props clawed noisily through the clouds. Suddenly, everything went black. The rain relented and began again, harder than before. Michael felt a tremulous shudder and knew they were approaching the eye wall, the deadliest part of the storm. The pitch of the propellers changed, and the Hercules began to slow.

The rain stopped as quickly as it had begun, and the shaking subsided. Once inside the eye, they sailed about in a strange calm with blue sky pouring in from above.

The Hercules was packing a special parcel. When released over its target, it would relay important data back to the National Hurricane Center in Miami. The dropsonde operator stood by, waiting for the word. Meanwhile, the plane made a couple of runs, searching for the storm's circulation center. When the airspeed and ground speed were in sync, the Weather Officer gave the order to release the dropsonde. The slender missile left its dispatch tube with ease and sailed toward the center of the storm.

CHAPTER 6

Hunting Island

Dew glistened atop the rounded roof of Jon Samuelson's decade-old Airstream, a bone thrown to him during a divorce turned ugly.

Inside the travel trailer, Samuelson stretched himself awake. He couldn't resist rising early, even on a self-proclaimed day off. Lately, he'd become keenly aware of the passage of time, clinging to each fleeting day.

His hands rose to his face. Thinking himself quite a sight, he felt his beard, growing since the day he left the Hurricane Center.

"You're just going through a mid-life crisis," had been his wife's initial observation. Samuelson knew better. He was hardly at the mid-life point and had never heard of anyone making it to the ripe old age of a hundred and twenty.

It wasn't really about age. He'd simply lost his tolerance for routine and bureaucracy, just woke up one morning and found it all pretty meaningless. He knew he could never endure another interminable meeting with the Department of Commerce or lengthy home remodel. His wife had insisted on his input, but in the end it was her choice. It had always been her choice.

During moments of honest reflection he liked to think he hadn't let her down, even in the end. She simply couldn't understand why he chose to leave the center without a fight. Swapping a comfortable lifestyle for a minimalist existence in order to pursue a life of self-funded weather research had seemed to her, unthinkable.

Samuelson shuffled through the trailer and ran some water into the sink. He splashed his face and finger-combed his gray hair into place before pulling on his wire-rims.

The coffee pot began to chug, and he took a seat at a cluttered table with a bowl of bran flakes and an overripe peach. Despite a failed marriage, there was much to be thankful for. His hand found a worn leather Bible on a nearby shelf. Inside, a half-dozen passages had been marked with the feathers of sea birds. He carved the peach into the bowl and mumbled a prayer, glancing skyward to see if anyone was listening.

After breakfast, he moved toward the radio and threw a rocker switch—alas, nothing but static. No weather reports waited in the tray beside the fax machine, so he toggled the power switch off and on for good measure.

Perhaps he'd call the Hurricane Center later and speak with Erik, try to confirm the storm's position. He missed their talks. After all, the hurricane specialist was his closest friend and the nearest thing he had to a son.

Across the trailer, vials of labeled core samples covered the counter. The coring contractor he'd hired on a part-time basis had gone to town the day before, for additional fuel and supplies. He wasn't due back until day after tomorrow, and there was little for Samuelson to do but grant himself a well-deserved day of rest. Aside from the sound of an occasional breaking wave, the island was extraordinarily quiet.

Seldom having time for the loneliness that would have consumed lesser men, he adjusted easily to life along the barrier islands.

He tore another page off the calendar and waited not-so-patiently for a coring permit to be granted in Columbia. Administrators at the University of South Carolina had unanimously approved his coring request on Pritchard's Island, and it was now up to the bureaucrats in the capital.

His work on Hunting Island was nearly finished. Pritchard's Island would be more challenging. The less accessible island was a favorite among marine biologists, and Samuelson felt certain its ancient sediments would yield even more clues about prehistoric storms.

After Pritchard's Island he planned to visit Edisto, Kiawah, Morris and Bull Islands. From there, he'd travel north to the Outer Banks. The irrefutable proof he'd spent a lifetime trying to find was nearly within his reach.

He swung open the trailer door and took in the sunrise. Overhead, a flock of noisy gulls sailed toward the mainland. Arlene had probably spun well into the Gulf by now, and it looked like another glorious day along the coast.

Samuelson remembered simpler times as a kid, up from Savannah with his father, surf-fishing every accessible strand from Garden City to Mt. Pleasant. A different prize brought him out to the barrier islands at this stage in his life, proof for a controversial weather theory.

It was a long step down to the damp asphalt where he stretched before following the breeze to the water's edge.

Along a frothy stretch of beach, waves of crazed mullet flittered ashore like bats beating from a cave. Hundreds of the small fish choked the shoreline, spooked from the shadows by the big drums charging up from the depths. Red choppers and drums, some called them channel bass. His eyes widened with the realization that the biggest fish prowled farther offshore. Nearby, a large fiddler crab made off with a stranded mullet and disappeared beneath a cabbage palm.

Back at the trailer, Samuelson grabbed a bucket and long-handled net before returning to the beach. He charged back across the sand, cuffed his pant legs and waited for the reds to run more bait fish into the shallows. Wading up to his calves, he caught a shimmering net of mullet and emptied them into the bucket.

After topping off the bucket with seawater, he headed for the launch ramp where he emptied the mullet into the boat's live well. Then it was back to the Airstream to pack a light lunch.

Inside of ten minutes he found himself heading east, small waves licking his stern. The morning clouds had dissipated, and the otherwise unremarkable sky began to take on a reddish glow.

Easing the throttle forward, he heard the engine purr and felt the spray against his face. Once beyond Fripp Island, he peeled off his glasses and wiped them against the lining of his sweatshirt—without them, everything looked a blur.

He pulled his glasses back on and lifted a pair of binoculars. Scanning the horizon, he observed a flock of seabirds working to the east. The mullet had apparently moved offshore, and Samuelson followed.

Up ahead he saw the old Hunting Island Light, the area's most prominent landmark. Despite its considerable size, even the lighthouse vanished in the mist. Losing one's way was exactly how mariners got into trouble, and Samuelson had no intention of getting lost out there. He put his faith in an internally gimbaled compass and a handheld GPS. He knew better than to be careless, and, boy, did he love his toys.

The logically laid-out helm consisted of a stainless steel wheel, Loran receiver perched slightly to the side, throttle to the right with a complement of gauges, including fuel level and alternator.

A marine-band radio was mounted at knee level just to the left of the helm, with an illuminated compass directly above and slightly behind the wheel.

He had even managed to find room for a small teak panel to the side of the instrument pod, bordered in braided rope. On it he had mounted a pair of tarnished brass instruments: a mariner's clock and a dented barometer perpetually stuck on fair weather since the day he bought it at a garage sale.

Samuelson stared disbelievingly at the barometer and blinked—something quite inexplicable had happened. The needle had swung all the way over to rain. Tapping the glass failed to dislodge the needle, and he figured there had either been a drastic drop in barometric pressure since he left Hunting Island or the instrument was malfunctioning.

He sniffed the sea air and shrugged, trusting his instincts instead. The barometer was obviously flawed. He tapped the instrument once more for luck and returned to the business of navigating. With his tank nearly full, he could run thirty miles offshore and back if he had to. A hot bite came along all too infrequently, and, mile after mile, he motored farther from shore.

By the time he finally caught up with the feeding birds, he had lost all sight of land. Gulls circled overhead and fish broke along the surface.

He fiddled with the Loran receiver. When the instrument failed to reckon his location, he tried the GPS. It was as if the boat's electronics had difficulty overcoming some powerful interference.

Samuelson glanced at the compass, then stared in the direction of where he'd last seen land. Moving aft, he checked the viability of the bait while diving sea birds hit the surface like kamikazes.

After nose-hooking a mullet, he flew the fish into a spot boiling with reds. Before he could count to four, a big fish slammed the bait. He waited three seconds, clicked on the drag and pumped the rod toward his chest, soundly setting the hook.

Round the boat the big fish swam, cutting left and right, taking more line with each run. After several long minutes, Samuelson felt his arms burn with fatigue. He finally managed to hoist the bass to the surface and watched it flap its broom-like tail.

The gaff found its mark, just beneath the gill plate. Using both hands, he lifted the huge fish onto the deck. Rivulets of blood ran aft through a pair of scuppers in the stern.

Exhausted, he fanned his face with his baseball cap and sat down to spread peanut butter on a heel of bread. A sip of iced cola helped wash it down.

He doused the bloody deck with a bucket of seawater and tried the radio: nothing but static. A quick check of the antennae wire revealed the possible culprit, metal contacts crusted with tell-tale green corrosion. Realizing he'd begun to let things go, Samuelson silently lectured himself about the virtues of maintenance, the sort of talking-to boys get from their fathers. Vowing to clean the contacts first thing upon his return, he chummed the surface with a fistful of lively bait.

Somewhere off the stern, a plastic bag floated inexorably toward the prop. It wrapped around the idling outboard and drew down flush against the suction of the water intake. The temperature began to rise until the overheated engine sputtered and died. Suddenly, an alarm sounded beneath the outboard's cowling.

Lunging toward the outboard, Samuelson tripped over the bass and spilled his soda on his way to the stern. When his foot hit a slimy patch of blood and scales, he went down hard. His chin struck the outboard, driving his front tooth into his lower lip.

His wire-rim glasses bounced from the ridge of his nose, hit the engine cowling and plunked into the sea. Grunting, he reached blindly underwater, praying his frantic fingers would find them. His tongue probed his parted lip and tasted the coppery blood oozing from it.

He pressed a paper towel firmly against the wound and sniffed the air. "Sonofabitch!"

The engine emitted the unmistakable burnt stink that equipment makes when real damage has been done. He tried the starter without luck and threw a switch to raise the prop. Bracing himself against the transom, he reached overboard until he felt the plastic bag wrapped soundly around the outboard's water intake.

After pulling the bag free, he tossed it behind the boat and tried the starter a second time—a puff of gassy smoke, a groan, that was all. He was stuck, and he knew it—well out of sight of land.

Adrift.

The wind developed a wicked howl, and his skin prickled with apprehension. Clouds filled the sky, casting an eerie darkness over the water.

Feeling very much alone, he weighed his limited options. His eyes detected walls of foam building along the surface. White caps, he thought, a sure sign of deteriorating weather. In less than an hour, his situation had gone from bad to unthinkable.

Beneath the dark canopy of the sky, the small boat pitched and yawed. Instinct and self-preservation took over as he felt the wind against his face, sustained and rising. He had a good nose for storms and smelled one coming.

His hand searched inside his right front pocket for the folding knife he kept there. Finding it, he reached beneath the console for the wires that delivered the power and radio signal. Feeling for corrosion, he unscrewed a pair of leads and saw sparks. Using the knife blade, he scratched down to bare metal and reattached the wires.

When a man finds himself in serious trouble he tends to know it. Samuelson knew this was true as he stared down the gray throat of potential disaster and recognized the danger, its growl low and menacing. For the first time in his life, he seriously feared the worst.

After he had been drifting for a time, he dug a sea anchor out from under the helm seat. He secured the anchor to a stern cleat and tossed it overboard.

The boat was tossed in the growing swell, and soon he had difficulty standing. He secured his life jacket and slid down against the upper edge of the port gunwale until seated on the fiberglass deck. Committed to staying with the boat no matter what, he drew his knees inward toward his chest and waited.

Finally, the sound of static and faint distorted voices crackled from the radio. Unable to read the luminous dial, he tried one channel after another until at last someone picked up his transmission, a shrimper out of Brunswick. It was the sound of a human voice, the sound of hope.

CHAPTER 7

Landfall

Earlier that morning, Erik awoke drenched in sweat. He'd been dreaming about his father again—they were poling around a shady swamp in a flat-bottomed skiff, baiting crayfish with strips of salt pork tied to strings.

Without warning, a thunderous roar exploded through the trees, and he called to his father in what seemed like slow motion.

Weaving his body skyward, Erik climbed the twisted branches of a dream tree and turned to offer his hand. His father remained just out of reach. A moment later, an enormous wave rumbled through the swamp and his father was gone.

Erik blinked twice at the plaster ceiling, confirming its existence. He heard the tick of an alarm clock and watched an overhead fan stir the air like an idling propeller. Breathing deep, he tried to slow his runaway heartbeat. It was the first time he'd had the nightmare in over a month.

He sat on the edge of the bed, resting his elbows on his knees and his head in his hands. He'd arrived back in Miami late the previous night and wasn't scheduled to return to work until after the weekend.

A faint buzzing came from the bedside table. Realizing he'd left his pager on vibrate mode, he switched the device to tonal. It beeped incessantly. With the push of a button he retrieved an urgent text message from the Hurricane Center: *RETURN TO CENTER ASAP.*

He killed the pager and whipped open the drapes. Up and down the boulevard, palm trees swayed in the easy breeze.

Several days had passed since Arlene had officially been classified as a tropical storm. Perhaps she'd matured into a full-blown hurricane. Or worse, she may have made landfall.

He pulled on a pair of faded jeans, a flannel shirt and grabbed his tote bag on his way out the door. His Saab fired up on the second try, and he raced past the botanicas and cigar shops on his way to I-836 and the Florida Turnpike. Traffic was unusually light, and he reached Florida International University in under twenty minutes, a personal best.

One look at the news vans surrounding the Hurricane Center and he knew something was shaking. It had to be something big, even the networks were out in force. A bus-sized newsmobile bearing Ocean Broadcasting's ubiquitous wave logo was parked out front with its antennae facing the sky.

The moment he blasted through the Center's doors, Heather stuck a microphone in his face. Gone were the polite formalities and fetching smile.

"Dr. Reynard, several days ago you said that the southeast coast faced no immediate danger from Arlene. Would you care to comment on the events of the last few hours? What's the center's official position now?"

"No comment," he said, spinning past her and shouldering through a mob of reporters blocking the foyer.

"Dr. Reynard?" she called, chasing after him. "Dr. Reynard!"

Relieved after reaching the other side of the crowded lobby, Erik glanced back at Heather over his shoulder.

She slapped her arms against her sides. "Damnit!"

Weaving his way through the labyrinth, he followed the hallway to a point where it turned and narrowed. The Center was packed with all the scientific talent Deevers could possibly muster.

Tai stopped him before he entered Tropical Analysis and Forecast Support. "I see you made it through the gauntlet."

"Looks like a slide rule convention around here."

"When was the last time you spoke to Samuelson?"

"What's he got to do with this?" Erik said, turning to Deevers.

"Nice of you to join us," the director said, momentarily muffling his cell phone. A second later, he was back on the line. "I want a Gulfstream brought in from Tampa, fueled and ready to go inside of an hour, comprende?"

"What the hell's going on?" Erik said.

"Goddam sun spots," Deevers said, punching a stout finger against his chest. "You, come with me."

Deevers sliced through the crowded room and paused just long enough to bark commands at a techie in a MENSA tee shirt.

Glancing at Tai, he said, "You ever seen one of these babies up close?"

"Not yet."

"Done any airborne storm reconnaissance?"

She shook her head.

"You've got to start sometime, Erik will fill you in on the drill."

They followed the director down a corridor leading toward an exit.

Erik said, "You still haven't told me what's going on."

"Arlene underwent a rapid deepening," Deevers said, "made landfall just before dawn."

"Where?"

"Savannah. Hit the coast like a runaway freight train, caught us totally unprepared. Solar anomalies have had our communications' people scrambling. Power's out all over the place, and the telephone lines are down. We had very little advance warning. Frankly, it's a big goddam mess."

"Did they manage an evacuation?"

"If you can call it that. Every road away from the coast is blocked with traffic, and at least one bridge is out. The Savannah River's backing up, and Routes 16 and 96 out of the city are parking lots. There's a lot of people going nowhere."

"How strong?" Erik asked.

"Winds north of one-twenty. Wilmington Island took the brunt of it. Afraid she's not showing much sign of letting up," Deevers added, mopping sweat from his forehead. "It doesn't look good."

"The press is ready for their update," a forecaster interrupted.

"Put Decker on it, and for God's sake keep those reporters out of here," Deevers said, hands rummaging around inside his pockets. "Christ, out of antacids. Reynard, you got anything for my stomach?"

"I don't take that stuff."

A few seconds later, a foil-wrapped roll sailed across the room. Deevers plucked the flying antacids out of the air and had a couple of chew-tabs in his mouth in nothing flat.

For Erik, the storm had reached a new category: potential killer.

"Savannah may get a break as the eye moves north."

"It's tracking north?" Erik said. "Has anyone spoken with Samuelson?"

"I thought you knew, the flippin' lines have been out for hours. Nobody's been able to get through."

A sour feeling fermented in Erik's gut like fast-setting concrete. No wonder Tai had asked about Samuelson. Surely he would have driven inland, away from the coast. Unless he didn't know about the storm's sudden deepening, and how could he have known? The Center didn't figure it out until it was too late to call for a proper evacuation.

"Nobody saw this coming?" Erik asked. "Toss me one of those antacids."

"Sunspots really did a job on our satellite communications. NASA's been reporting strong solar and geomagnetic activity for days. What I really need is to get firsthand observers on the ground. That's where the two of you come in. Grab your gear and follow me."

"Are you coming"

"Only as far as the airport, I've got a day's worth of meetings in Washington. Congress probably wants to find out what we're doing about the drought."

"As if anything can be done," said Erik.

Deevers pushed though a pair of exterior doors and raised the collar of his overcoat. "They picked a hell of a time for a meeting. Washington's so ill-informed, they probably think the southern oscillation's a new dance craze."

Tai dashed to her car and joined them a few minutes later with a small overnight bag slung over her shoulder.

"I'll see the two of you as far as Georgia, assuming we get clearance to land, that is. You'll be met on the ground by a team from FEMA, they'll take you into Savannah."

The entourage moved quickly across the parking lot toward a cream-colored Ford sedan with government plates.

"Catch," Deevers said, tossing the keys to Erik, "you drive." He spun toward Tai, punched a number into his cell phone and handed it to her. "You're on with the tower. See if they've secured clearance for us to land."

Erik lowered the hood of his coat and turned the key. Under more favorable circumstances, he could imagine vacationing in Savannah, maybe taking in a round of golf. Still, something gnawed at him—NOAA's lack of an advance warning simply didn't make sense.

A faded deodorizer strip in the shape of a pine tree dangled from the rearview mirror, and three cigar butts crowded the sedan's ashtray.

Tai slid into the back seat. Deevers draped his coat between the seats and sat shotgun, an unlit cigar between his lips before the door swung shut. Erik took one look and hoped he had no intention of smoking the damn thing.

Tai soundproofed her free ear with the tip of her finger and spoke, a series of uh-huhs into the cellular. She scratched some notes into a flip pad and said, "Thanks sugar," to someone on the other end of the line.

Erik caught her eye in the rearview mirror and winked. This was Tai's first major hurricane, an initiation of sorts.

"Well?" Deevers said, turning toward the back seat.

"Charleston's a no go. They can get us clearance into Columbia, maybe Augusta."

The director's eyes flashed back and forth, as if his options were lined up on the dash.

"Get the tower back on the line. Tell them to clear us into Augusta—then notify FEMA, tell them we're on our way."

Erik felt the adrenaline kick in. Everything was happening fast. From Savannah it would be a short hop to Hunting Island, Samuelson's last known address.

CHAPTER 8

Savannah

The grand old city struggled back to her feet in the hours immediately following the storm. She'd held up admirably under the onslaught, despite the lack of an advance warning.

Inside the Civil Defense shelter, damage assessments were being compiled. Outside, Erik spotted an all too familiar banner, a single red cross on a field of white. The agency had arrived at the disaster scene early, setting up shop at a local school and converting a gymnasium into temporary housing for displaced victims.

After meeting with a roomful of officials from the Chatham Emergency Management Association beneath the old courthouse on Bull Street, they hiked across the storm-littered asphalt and jumped into a Suburban with government plates.

They hadn't traveled far when the Suburban slowed to a stop outside police headquarters at Haversham and Oglethorpe. They were met by the chief of police and several administrative types.

The chief studied Erik, letting his eyes linger on his shoulder-length hair.

"You must be Reynard?"

"That's right," Erik said. "Sorry we got here so late."

"You feel like being sorry about something, be sorry we didn't get an advance warning. What the hell are you people doing down there, anyway?"

"I've been in Houston," Erik said, realizing the excuse was

of little help. "A major communications' link went on the fritz due to solar activity—sunspots, that sort of thing."

"Nice old building," Tai interjected. "What do you call it?"

"I call it the office," the chief said, starting down the hall.

"I mean what style, architecturally speaking?"

"Savannah Gray Brick."

"But it's red?"

"I noticed," he said, leading them inside. "People around here been run pretty hard. We had a damn tough night. From the looks of it, the worst is over—at least I pray it is. We operated out of the Civil Defense Center beneath the courthouse most of the night. I understand you just came from there."

Erik nodded. "We flew into Augusta before noon and surveyed damage along the way."

"It's a hell of a mess. Not much looting, I'm happy to say. Just pray some of the missing manage to show." The chief turned to a gray-haired woman. "Helen, how many still unaccounted for?"

"Down to fourteen," she said with a hopeful smile, "those that we know of."

The chief stroked his chin and turned to Erik. "We cleared out a conference room for you and the FEMA team. The folks from Chatham Emergency Management will be along shortly."

Erik and Tai made their way down a tiled hallway. Continued flooding along the debris-choked Savannah River remained one of their gravest concerns. It was water that did the real damage.

After meeting with local emergency personnel, they continued down the crowded hall. Erik felt a tug at his arm and turned around to face a man in overalls.

"Hey, mister, you seen my son?"

The man reached into his pocket and withdrew a small photograph. Erik held the picture to the light—it featured a small boy in a Cub Scout uniform seated on a green and yellow tractor. This was the part of the job that stung.

"Sorry," Erik said, "I haven't seen him. Tell you what, though, I'll keep an eye out. What's his name?"

"Noah," the man replied, his face drawn up tight. "Noah

Clements. He was on a sleep-over when the wind came up."

"That's a good strong name," Erik said, patting the man's shoulder. "He'll be fine, I'm sure of it."

"Four miscarriages before the lord blessed us with a child. No way my wife could go through that again. You gotta help us find our boy."

Erik felt all wormy inside. He couldn't help but think the lack of a warning was somehow his fault, even though he knew better.

"Deputy started bangin' on the door at midnight," the man went on. "Told us we had to evacuate. We left everything behind but our coats and wallets."

"Your son's probably just as worried about you," Erik said.

The man smiled halfheartedly and gave his wife a reassuring hug. Her eyes were dark and tired, like she hadn't slept in days.

Up ahead, a crowd milled around the police department's entrance with blankets draped over their shoulders, sipping coffee from Styrofoam cups. Erik led Tai toward the lobby.

"This is pathetic," she whispered, heading out the door. "Those poor people."

"It gets to you if you let it," he said. "Don't worry, he'll find his son." "Most of the missing will be accounted for once the phones come back up, but not everyone. Arlene's a killer, I could see that right away. Some of the missing will wash up later along the beach, bloated with gas. They'll call out the K-9 units. Dogs usually find them. It's still too early to get an assessment of casualties."

Tai grimaced. "No more details, okay?"

Erik agreed, and they rejoined their FEMA counterparts back out in the street. They passed a section of downtown resembling a war zone and opted to head for Augusta before a mandated curfew went into effect.

CHAPTER 9

Rendezvous

The Suburban whisked along Interstate 20, all the way into Augusta. Erik stared out the side window, unable to shake the image of the distraught couple he'd met back in Savannah.

After plowing through a flooded intersection, they headed toward a Marriott Courtyard sign. FEMA's Dwight Moffett was at the wheel. Erik sat shotgun, cuffing the passenger window for a better view. In the rear seat, Tai fiddled with her phone, checking for messages. Beside her sat Bud Van Kampen, also with FEMA, scanning a clipboard with a flashlight.

"Here we are," said Dwight.

Erik entered the hotel lobby behind Tai. It was a far cry from the devastation they had observed back in Savannah. Unbuttoning his coat, he watched impatient travelers wait uneasily in a long serpentine line winding around inside the lobby.

Dwight Moffett and Bud Van Kampen came in from the weather a few moments later. They bypassed the lobby and headed straight for the lounge, appearing remarkably unconcerned about securing lodging for the night.

"I hope we get rooms," Erik said, watching the FEMA crew shuttle past.

Tai lowered the hood of her foul weather slicker and blew the hair out of her face. Her fingers worked the zipper of her bag and removed a round compact. It opened with a click, and she stared at her reflection in the mirror. "That's attractive," she said and closed it.

"You've just been through a hurricane, remember? Once

we check in, why don't you join me for a nightcap? I hate drinking alone."

"Honey, what I need is a warm bath and a soft pillow."

Erik smiled an obligatory smile and struggled for honesty in his own self assessment. He did drink alone—most nights, really. It seldom interfered with his performance at work—he was far too controlled to ever let that happen. A couple of drinks tended to stop the nightmares and quiet the complex machinery of his mind.

Suddenly, a commotion flared at the front of the line. A man began shouting obscenities when he learned there were no more rooms, and it appeared the overworked hotel clerk might have a riot on her hands.

Erik had seen this sort of thing before. He knew the signs. Everyone had a breaking point, and he felt sorry for the clerk. No doubt she'd rather be home with her family on such a night. The man's face reddened, and he sent a stack of brochures flying with a sudden sweep of his arm.

The wind howled, lights flickered and the troublesome man stormed outside. Back inside the lobby, stranded travelers let out an audible sigh of collective relief.

Erik said, "How do you feel about sleeping in the Suburban?"

"Don't tell me they're full up. Are there any other hotels around here?"

"Beats me."

Tai stared outside. "That guy really lost it."

"Disasters tend to do that, people sometimes go a little nuts."

Dwight Moffett left the company of the hotel manager and called them over. "We've got rooms."

"What about them?" Erik protested, motioning over his shoulder at the flock of turned-away travelers.

"One of the benefits of being federal employees."

Although thankful for a place to sleep, Erik thought it sucked. What gave them the right to move ahead of the rest?

"There's one slight problem," Dwight added, stepping forward with a single card key. "You'll have to share a room."

Before Erik could refuse, Tai thrust out her hand. "I'll take that."

Not a word was spoken as they moved up the stairs and down the carpeted corridor. Erik didn't understand why he had difficulty sharing a room. After all, they were adults, and he'd known Tai for nearly a year. Still, he felt relieved when the door opened to reveal a pair of full-sized beds.

He gave the room the once over—theft-proof hangers, room service menu and the all important television guide. He flopped onto the bed Tai hadn't staked out and perused the menu. Perhaps he'd order a midnight snack after checking out the lounge.

He reached for the phone, dialed nine for an outside line and tried the Hurricane Center in Miami. A robotic voice chimed in, declining to complete the call due to high call volume. The storm continued to take its toll.

A second attempt, this time to reach Samuelson, produced a similar result. Erik thought about his friend, hoping he'd made the decision to move to higher ground. The barrier islands were low stretches of land, and the effect of a significant storm surge would have been devastating.

A few minutes later, the bathroom door creaked open, and a puff of mysterious steam preceded Tai through the opening. In less than ten minutes she'd managed to transform herself—silk blouse tapered at the waist and flaring slightly over her slender hips, black slacks, hair combed back and gathered beneath a gold clip.

"It's all yours," she said

"I'm glad you decided to join me."

She held up a single index finger. "One drink."

Not to be outdone, Erik swapped into a fresh pair of Levis, gray sweatshirt and sneakers.

He slipped the card key into his wallet and held the door open with his foot. "After you."

The lounge was small, but in proper balance with the one-hundred-thirty room inn—mellow music, woodsy atmosphere and manicured landscape beyond ample windows. Erik followed his colleague toward an out-of-the-way table.

"So this is what storm chasing's all about."

"Sometimes," he said, scooting a chair behind her. "It

beats struggling through hip-deep water with electric lines spark-ing overhead and the wind blowing so hard you can barely stand."

They ordered drinks—she a brandy, he a Bloody Mary.

"About tomorrow," she said, "what's the plan?"

"I want you to stay here at the hotel, close to the phone. I've got a little errand to run."

"Searching for Samuelson?" she said. "Well, I'm coming, too. You can't just ditch me here."

"No way. You're staying here to mind the farm. Deevers will want a full assessment."

"And what if he wants to speak with you?"

"Tell him something...tell him anything, just keep him out of my hair."

"If I do stay behind, you're going to owe me big time."

"Deal."

Something or someone caught Tai's attention, and she rose with her brandy. She took a healthy swig and said, "I'll be up in the room."

"Retiring so early?"

"Looks like you've got company," she said, motioning to an approaching blonde. She leaned close and whispered, "Don't let your eyes get your ass in trouble."

Erik cringed when Tai bumped into the reporter, spilling her drink. Heather regained her composure and reached his table with an empty glass.

"What's with your friend?" she said, wiping the front of her wine-soaked blouse.

"Must have been an accident."

"Trust me, it was no accident."

Heather scanned the wine list and ordered the best Napa Cabernet the hotel served by the glass. At least it was the most expensive.

"What's new on the storm front," she said.

"Oh, no," he said, waggling his index finger back and forth. "I tried being chummy with you before and look where it got me."

"I was just doing my job. Look, this storm's news, and so are you."

"The storm may be news, but me? I'm afraid you're mis-taken."

"I've been doing a little research—I had no idea you were so well respected."

"Go on," he said.

"What can you tell me about Dr. Samuelson?"

Whoa, where had she heard that name? Stalling, he mixed his drink with a swizzle stick and took a sip. "He was my boss, left the Hurricane Center and took his research on the road."

"Voluntary move?"

"Let's just say he had a little run-in with the Weather Czar."

Erik flagged down the cocktail waitress and ordered another round.

"What kind of run-in?"

"Look, I don't know if I should be talking to you."

"How about off the record?" she said. "Just between us?"

"We have an Office of Public Affairs and media people back in Miami. Why don't you interrogate them?"

"I didn't know I was bothering you," she said, rising slowly to her feet.

"Sorry, I didn't mean that."

"Apology accepted," she said, easing back into the chair.

"What brings you to Augusta?"

"I was on my way to Washington to cover a Congressional meeting, but got stuck here instead. I'm scheduled to fly out in the morning."

"You're not here to cover the storm?"

"My editor took me off the weather desk and reassigned me to the political beat. He sent me down to the Hurricane Center this morning as a follow-up. Tonight, when I saw you sitting here, I wanted to apologize for being so pushy."

"Sure you're not sniffing around for a story?"

"Relax, anything you tell me is between friends," she said, scooting close.

"Totally off the record?"

"Scout's honor," she said.

"What would you like to know? It's not like we're working on classified doomsday weapons down at the Center."

"For starters, I'd like to know what possesses a Louisiana farm boy to become the world's leading authority on hurricanes?"

"School came easy to me. I received my Bachelor of Science from Tulane."

"At seventeen, I understand."

"Sounds like you already know quite a bit about me. What else do you know?"

"Let's see, you were born in the bayous of rice and cane farmer stock. You showed considerable scientific aptitude at an early age, building your first shortwave set at ten and passing your Novice Class, Ham radio exam at eleven. You're also an outspoken environmentalist who steers clear of committees, preferring to work alone."

"You've got the ball," he said. "Let's see you run with it."

"You received your doctorate at MIT, top of your class, I might add, then served research stints in Antarctica and the Amazon Basin before joining NOAA, where you met and began working with Dr. Samuelson."

"We immediately hit it off, he's been like a father. How'd you find out so much about me, anyway?"

"Reporters have to protect their sources."

"Not if they want to continue the interview."

"Hometown newspapers are good places to start. So tell me, what does your father think about your paternal bond with Samuelson?"

Recognizing there was a gap in her assessment of his life, Erik sucked down the last of his drink. "I doubt if he thinks much about it. He died before my eleventh birthday."

"Sorry."

The waitress brought another round, and he promptly spiked his drink with a splash of Tabasco.

"Nobody lives forever," he added, coolly.

Realizing it was an odd, insensitive thing to say, he wanted to swallow his words. He missed his father, deeply. Perhaps no one did live forever, but that didn't mean they deserved to go like that, to drown in a storm.

Heather slid her chair close, until her thigh touched his.

"Where's Samuelson now?" she said.

"He's living in a travel trailer, doing weather research. I'm heading out to see him tomorrow. He hasn't been heard from in a week."

"Why don't you tell me about his interest in paleoclimatology?" She moved her lips close to his ear and whispered, "Totally off the record."

Unclear if it was the vodka, the narcotic effect of her perfume or the close proximity of her perfect mouth—Erik held out valiantly for three or four seconds before giving in. "He's got this theory about the weather, claims the Earth's simply going through a natural cycle, one that repeats every thousand millennia. The changes are beginning to accelerate, and..."

"And?" she prodded, her finger rounding the lip of her wine glass.

"His research turned up something, fossilized proof of prehistoric superstorms. According to Samuelson, it's all there in the geologic record, evidence of hurricanes so strong they defy all atmospheric models."

Heather parked her chin on folded hands as if caught in the rapture of a suspenseful tale. "How strong?"

Erik looked around and whispered, "Storms powerful enough to lay waste entire nations."

"Why doesn't the government warn people about the danger?"

"That's a very good question."

"But if you knew a storm was imminent, you'd have no choice, right? I mean, people do have a right to know."

"Imminent is the operative word," he said. "If I knew with certainty, sure I'd go public with it—I'd have to."

"Even if it meant your job?"

"Absolutely."

Erik fished a pen out of his jeans and dabbed it against a cocktail napkin. "The Saffir-Simpson Scale works like this— storms are ranked according to their pressure, wind speed and surge."

He drew a vertical column of ascending numbers from one to five. Across the top he wrote category, pressure, wind and surge.

"What about Hurricane Arlene?" she asked.

He counted down three columns and ran his finger across the napkin.

"She's a Category 3 storm, central pressure measuring 950

millibars, winds of one-twenty and nine-foot surge. Make no mistake, she's a serious storm. Fewer than two Category 3 hurricanes make landfall every three years."

Her eyes drifted to the bottom of the napkin, to the last box. "What about those?"

"That's Category 5 territory, the most destructive. Widespread structural failures, eighteen-foot surge and wind speeds over a hundred-fifty-five miles per hour. On average, only about one Category 5 hurricane makes landfall per century."

"That's a relief."

"Not entirely, three Atlantic hurricanes have reached Category 5 strength since 1988—so much for averages."

"And that explains Samuelson's fascination with monster storms?"

"He's been evaluating prehistoric silt and pollen deposited along the barrier islands and finds clues in the core samples he collects. Years ago, he tried to warn a world weather conference about the relationship between severe storms and global warming."

"What happened?"

"He failed to prove a correlation."

"I'm sure they'd listen to him now," she said, "given the severity of the drought."

"That's not the least of it. We've got vanishing fish habitats in the tropics, cholera epidemics erupting in South America and outbreaks of malaria in the highlands of Rwanda. This isn't just about hurricanes—the weather's changing."

He unfolded a second napkin and sketched her profile. Heather approved with a smile.

"So, is there a Mr. Conroy out there somewhere, maybe a gaggle of kids?"

Just as she was about to answer, the waitress made her rounds, collecting glasses. "We'll be closing in about five minutes. Y'all have a nice night."

Promptly forgetting the unanswered question, Erik went for his wallet.

"Might as well put that away," the waitress said. "Your friend took care of the bill."

"Tonight's on me," Heather said with a wink.

He wasn't accustomed to having beautiful women buy him drinks, but he quickly warmed to the idea.

Reaching down to retrieve the cocktail napkins, he noticed they were gone.

"Coming?" Heather asked.

Erik wavered to his full height and followed her up the stairs. They reached the point where the corridors split at a crossroads and stopped.

"I'd love to hear more about Samuelson's research," she said, polishing the banister with her palm. "Feel like coming in?"

She didn't have to ask him twice. Once inside the hotel room, she unbuttoned her cuffs, pulled the tail of her blouse out of her skirt and kicked her pumps into the closet.

"Make yourself comfortable," she said. "I want to get out of these wet clothes."

Moon-eyed, he leaned back on the bed and let his head sink into the pillow. He could see the narrow curve of her back in a wall-mounted mirror and watched her slip into an oversized pajama top.

Slowly, the room began to turn. He closed his eyes and listened to the rain lash the window. Beyond the rain, he heard the distant rumble of thunder. Alone with a beautiful woman in the midst of a storm—wasn't life grand?

CHAPTER 10

The morning after

Erik awoke to the incessant racket of a jackhammer and the whine of a far-off siren. He bolted upright and whipped open the drapes. A glance at the digital clock on the nightstand confirmed the time, a little past eight.

The events of the previous night came inching back. He remembered being with Heather—she'd invited him up for a drink. But from that point on, the evening blurred.

On the pillow beside him lay a red rose and a note. In it, she thanked him for an enjoyable evening and apologized for having to run. She promising to stay in touch and asked him to think of her, always.

Erik looked around for his shoes and found them paired neatly at the foot of the bed. He wondered what had happened the night before and what memories he'd been robbed of. Detecting a hint of perfume on his shirt, he was pretty sure of one thing—bumping into Heather was no accident.

When he returned to his room, he found Tai sitting on the edge of her bed, legs crossed, nibbling a bit of dry toast. The television blared.

"Turn down the TV," he said, "the volume's killing my head."

"About time you showed," she said, lowering the volume on the remote, "hope she was worth it."

"Do you have any aspirin?"

"In my bag," she said, tossing it onto his bed.

"We talked all night, I sort of lost track of the time."

"Please," she said. "I wasn't born yesterday."

Erik peeled off his sweatshirt on his way to the bathroom. "Like I said, it was a long night."

"Better get moving if you plan to find Samuelson."

A few minutes later, he stepped from the bathroom, working a clean shirt into his jeans.

"Did Moffett call about the keys?"

"He left them at the front desk and said you can keep the Suburban as long as needed. Call the FEMA field office when you're finished."

"Any word from our beloved leader?"

"See for yourself," she said, punching up the volume.

Suddenly, Erik remembered Deevers' whereabouts. He snatched a piece of toast from the room service tray when Tai wasn't looking and watched the President approach a podium.

"Maybe we can spot him in the crowd," he said, scooting close for a better look.

But the camera didn't leave the President. He spoke about the drought and lamented the menacingly high interest rates, a consequence of skyrocketing grain prices.

"This ought to be good," Erik said, stuffing a foul weather slicker into his duffel bag. I can't wait to hear what he plans to do about the weather."

"Like something can be done," she added.

"They should have listened to Samuelson," Erik said. "He had it right all along."

"A lot of good it's done him."

"At least he stands up for what he believes."

"Honey, if that's what standing up gets you, I'm keeping my mouth shut. Dining on rice and steamed fish out on some island isn't exactly my idea of making it."

"It's not so bad," Erik said, his eyes returning to the television.

There, seated with a contingent from the Department of Weather, was Deevers. Erik could tell by his gleaming head and bored expression. For an instant the camera actually lingered on him, just long enough to catch the sonofabitch yawning.

"Did you see that?"

Tai glanced back at the television. "What'd I miss?"

"Classic Deevers, yawning on national television, in the middle of the President's speech."

They looked at each other and laughed.

"We will meet the situation head-on," said the President, "and bring an end to the current weather crisis."

Erik shook his head. "It'll take more than installing a hack like Bobby Ocean."

"Give him some credit. He built Ocean Broadcasting from scratch."

"He's a TV weatherman, for Christ's sake. Probably a real Boy Scout, too."

"Do I detect a bit of jealousy? Just because he jets around with the Hollywood set..."

"I don't care who he jets around with. All I'm saying is, I doubt if he's the most qualified person for the job. Besides, you ever wonder why someone like Ocean bothers to serve as a Cabinet secretary? It can't be the money, there's got to be an angle."

"Service to his country?"

"Don't be so naïve."

"At least I'm not cynical."

Erik paused near the door. "I'm a pragmatist."

"What you are is impossible. Now get out of here, and quit eating my toast."

CHAPTER 11

On the road

Erik located the Suburban at the far end of the hotel parking lot. The FEMA seal on the door was a dead giveaway: a white triangle inside a black circle, floating above an eagle's head.

There was a stiffness to the wind, and he hoped Hunting Island had fared better than Savannah. Consulting a folding map he found above the visor, he located the intersection of I-95 near Old House and placed a quick call to the State Police to check for road closures. Anxious to catch up with the fast-moving storm, he got into the easy rhythm of the road and pushed the Suburban past seventy.

Outside of Beaufort, the traffic slowed to a crawl near a National Guard checkpoint. Horns blared, and a line of cars were turned away. Erik swung onto the shoulder and raced toward the front of the line where he found himself staring down the barrel of an M-16. The guardsman spotted his government plates, then lowered his gun and waved him through.

On the opposite side of the road, a truck-crane fished a school bus out of a flooded ditch, no doubt a casualty of the storm. He idled past the accident scene and glanced into his rearview mirror, praying the bus's occupants had made it to safety.

Trees swayed in the gathering blow, leaves flashing silver and green. He sensed a change in the wind and channel-surfed the radio until he found a local weather report. Moments later, heavy rain began to fall.

The last time he'd been out to the South Carolina coast, Samuelson was behind the wheel. This time, nothing looked familiar. He squinted through the rain, wondering if he'd taken a wrong turn.

Switching the wipers to high, he spotted a small country store off to the side of the road. He slowed the Suburban to a crawl. Rain gushed from channels in the building's tin roof, and the makeshift chimney leaned.

After pulling off the road, he parked beneath a sign advertising beer, ice and bait. Across the gravel lot, a man in a yellow raincoat hunched over a fallen tree with an idling chain saw in his hands.

Rain trickled down Erik's cheek, and he lifted his collar on his way up the steps to the store. To the left of the door stood a cabinet brimming with Styrofoam bait cups. He gazed through the darkened window and turned the doorknob.

The jingle of an overhead bell preceded his entry. A few moments later the storekeeper followed him inside with a flickering lantern in his hand. He sported a short white beard, eyes glowing like bits of ivory set in smiling ebony.

About the store, baskets woven from sweetgrass and strips of palmetto leaf held herbal teas, plastic lighters, fish hooks and sinkers, cigarette rolling papers and an assortment of local produce. A corner cooler advertised beer, milk and wine. To the side of the register a sheet of plywood covered a blown-out window.

The storekeeper's lips parted to expose the few remaining teeth dotting his friendly smile. "Help you find something?"

"Cup of coffee, if it's not too much trouble."

"Only takes a minute," he said, lighting the stove with a wooden match. "Have a look around."

Erik wandered around the dimly lit store, taking in the scent of cedar and kerosene. "Slow day?"

"I'll say," he said, letting his nose linger over a fresh tin of coffee.

Erik motioned outside. "What happened to those trees?"

"Tornado touched down during the storm." Reaching his hand over the counter, the storekeeper said, "I'm Lucas Butler, friends call me Luke."

"Erik," Reynard said, shaking the old man's hand. "I'm

from the N.H.C."

The acronym was met with a blank stare.

"The Hurricane Center, down in Miami."

"National Guard ain't been letting too many people by this way, I figured you was somebody."

"I'm surveying hurricane damage, looking for a friend of mine, too. Maybe you know him," Erik said, "name's Samuelson, Dr. Jon Samuelson."

The storekeeper scratched his beard, as if searching for some lost thought.

"Stands about five-nine, sixties, gray beard, glasses—fact is, he looks a lot like that," Erik said, shuffling toward a montage of fishermen taped to a rusty freezer. "Top row, far right."

It was Samuelson all right, kneeling in front of a respectable pile of fish.

"Sure, I know him. That's Doc, plays a mean game of checkers."

The storekeeper filled two mugs. He poured a jolt from a hipflask and slid the virgin mug over to Erik.

"Snake juice," Luke said with a grin. "Care for a nip?"

Erik declined. He brought the coffee to his lips and sipped, relieved they were getting somewhere. "Great coffee."

"Succory root, helps draw out the bitters." The storekeeper sorted through a box of mail destined for the post office and lifted a taped-up parcel wrapped in brown paper. "Might as well save the postage, looks like this one's meant for you."

Erik weighed the package in his hands and read the return address. It was from Samuelson.

"That storm came up quick, without a lick of warning. Came screaming through here like a banshee, a damned unholy sound."

"When did you last see Samuelson?"

"Day or so ago, before the storm. Keeps his trailer out on Hunting Island. Hope he got out okay."

"Me, too," Erik said, lifting a necklace from a nearby basket.

"They're six bucks apiece, or two for ten."

Polishing an inlaid stone with his thumb, Erik studied a vortex etched in its surface.

"Old Mary carves them out of soapstone. She's into all sorts of magic, claims they're lucky. Course, if you saw that shack she calls home, you might argue just how lucky they are." The storekeeper shrugged. "Good sellers, all the same."

"I'll take one," Erik said, slipping the talisman over his head.

What he really wanted was something for the throbbing in his frontal lobe, the price he paid for the excesses of the previous night. After tossing a tin of aspirin onto the counter, he settled up and consulted a wall map.

"Follow U.S. 21 to the end, you can't miss it. If you see Samuelson, tell him his crab is in."

CHAPTER 12

Aftermath

A quick search of his wallet yielded a folded note, containing Samuelson's hand-written directions. Keeping one hand on the wheel, Erik tossed his wallet onto the seat beside him.

By the time he reached the storm-battered entrance to Hunting Island State Park, a nervous sensation began to radiate from a point just below his navel. The Suburban rolled slowly toward a barricade which appropriately read *park closed.*

He'd been out to the island before, but he was totally unprepared for what he found. Gone were the campers and motor homes, nothing but devastation for as far as he could see. He idled ahead, as if exploring some inhospitable alien landscape—hard to believe it was the same island he'd visited several weeks earlier.

The Suburban dug in like a dozer, through the jungle of mud and shredded vegetation. Erik slowed to a stop near the campsites, pulled on a pair of rubber boots and stepped outside into the muck. Off in the distance, he thought he recognized something.

The glint of metal glistened up ahead, a barely identifiable heap. Moving closer, he noticed a shredded canvas awning flapping along the ground. It was Samuelson's trailer all right. Judging from its condition, moving the Airstream out of harm's way appeared to have been the last thing on Samuelson's mind. This observation suggested several scenarios, none of them good.

The rising wind brought a fast-moving curtain of rain.

Erik inched ahead, wondering what had happened. The Airstream's back was broken—its windows, burst. Aluminum ribs poked through the metallic skin of the trailer like compound fractures, wheels half-buried in sludge, branches and leaves.

He shimmied up the rounded roof of the overturned trailer and bellied toward the door. Taking hold of the latch, he prayed he wouldn't find his friend inside. He flung open the door and let it drop with a crash.

The air rising from the opening smelled of dampness and wet paper. His eyes traced every inch of the interior: no body, no blood and no sign of Samuelson. Where in the hell was he?

Erik came up for air and stared out at the stormy sea. He had nearly given up on finding his friend when he spotted a pickup truck and empty boat trailer parked near the launch ramp. Sitting quietly atop the Airstream, he studied the troubling silhouette in the distance. It looked like Samuelson's truck, but where was the boat? Find it, he thought, and he would likely find his friend.

Inside the Airstream a few things had somehow managed to stay dry. He lowered himself through the opening and fell the last foot or so into the muck.

A half-dozen books had miraculously come to rest atop an upside down file cabinet. One of the books caught his eye, a leather-bound copy of the King James Bible with the feathers of seabirds wedged between its pages. He found Samuelson's signature inside—the signature of a child, jerky and unpracticed.

Erik respectfully brushed debris from the book's worn cover and opened it to a page marked by a single feather, the book of Psalms. The page had been further annotated with passages underlined in pencil. His fingers traced down the page, finding nearly illegible notations scribbled in the margins.

For he commandeth, and raiseth the stormy wind, which lifteth up the waves thereof.

Strange, he thought, Samuelson's secret penchant for the Bible. Occasionally, he would get hold of some philosophical point with the tenacity of a Nile crocodile. More than one bureaucrat from the Department of Commerce had made the mistake of going one on one with Samuelson, only to be dragged down the slippery bank of logic.

Erik flipped through more pages, stopping at another feather marker.

And the rain descended, and the floods came, and the winds blew, and beat upon that house; and it fell; and great was the fall of it.

His friend had apparently come to a spiritual crossroads while out in the islands. It wasn't uncommon for scientists to go a bit mad from time to time. Some found peace in religion, some in study and some in a bottle. Samuelson had resigned himself from the rat race, from marriage and commitments, at the edge of an angry sea.

Erik reached up and slid the Bible safely atop the trailer. Returning to the overturned file cabinet, he was shocked to find its drawers empty. Where were Samuelson's research journals and his precious core samples? He seldom let them out of his sight.

As he hoisted himself back through the doorway, he heard the wail of a siren, so close it rattled the windows. A Ford patrol vehicle pulled up beside the trailer with its red, blue and amber lights flashing.

An officer dressed in a foul weather poncho moved toward him, running his hand down his side as if checking for his gun. He spat in the mud. "Park's closed."

Erik slid down the wall of the toppled trailer and sized up the deputy who looked to be on the south side of thirty.

"Is that your vehicle?" the deputy asked, motioning toward the Suburban.

"It's a loaner," Erik said, reaching for the photo ID he kept in his wallet.

The deputy drew his weapon. "Hands up and turn around, nice and easy."

"I was just going for my..."

"Shuddup, and lace your fingers behind your head."

Erik did as he told and felt the deputy swing in close.

"They said someone might show."

"What are you talking about?"

"Don't remember asking you a damn thing," said the officer.

Without warning, the deputy threw his forearm between Erik's shoulder blades and knocked him toward the front of the Suburban. He bent Erik over the hood and kicked his legs apart.

The deputy was breathing hard. "Stay down," he warned as he slipped inside the Suburban.

Erik felt the warmth of the engine against his cheek and watched raindrops turn to steam. Staring out of one eye, he watched the deputy rummage around inside the vehicle, through his zippered bag and beneath the seats. Finding nothing of criminal interest, his search became more frantic.

Stay calm, Erik told himself, play it cool—give the deputy's blood chemistry a chance to normalize. An important arrest out in the islands would probably earn him a commendation. He silently fantasized bringing so much heat down on the overly zealous deputy that he'd likely pull parking patrol until eligible for his pension.

The deputy returned several minutes later and emptied the contents of his wallet onto the hood. He lifted a Florida license and said, "You're a long ways from Miami, Mister..."

"Doctor," Erik corrected, "Dr. Reynard."

The deputy holstered his weapon. "Are you with FEMA?"

"I'm with the National Hurricane Center," Erik said.

The deputy didn't look up—he just kept going through his wallet. He found a laminated ID issued by the Department of Weather and lifted it for a better look.

A knot of pain bloomed between Erik's shoulder blades where he'd been forearmed, and he turned his stare on the deputy. "I borrowed the Suburban from a FEMA crew down in Savannah, drove out here looking for a friend of mine. You can check it out if you'd like. I've got the FEMA number here in my pocket."

The officer's face went pale. "Sorry I roughed you up, but you don't look like a federal employee."

"Who's the sheriff around here?"

The deputy stuttered out a name and said, "Can't be too careful. We've had several reports of looters. That fella from the Department of Weather told me this trailer was off limits and to be on the lookout."

"What'd he look like?"

"Blonde hair, thirties—sounded foreign, German maybe." The deputy glanced down, as if more answers could be found in the mud. "Came prepared, too, slipped on a pair of hip-waders and had a look inside the trailer. He was still in there when I left."

"What was he driving?"

"That's easy," said the deputy, "a brand new Hummer, a shiny black one."

"I don't suppose you caught his name."

"His ID said Department of Weather, same as yours. That was good enough for me. Like I said, he warned me to keep an eye on the trailer. Next thing I knew, you drove up."

Erik felt his blood pressure rise. He had other things on his mind, like finding his friend.

"What do you suppose the sheriff's gonna say when I tell him you had nothing better to do in the hurricane's wake than waste my time, shakin' me down, while I was stuck on this mud spit conducting official business?" Erik swung his stare out to sea. "Does your department have a patrol boat?"

"It's over on Hilton Head. They hauled her out for maintenance. Once the sea calms down, she'll be back in service."

Erik trudged toward the Airstream. He moved along the trailer's length and let his fingers brush the rounded roofline.

"Sure is a lot of interest in that trailer," the deputy said, gazing in the direction of the launch ramp. "By the way, I ran the plates on that pickup."

"Let me guess," Erik said, "it's registered to Jon Samuelson, right?"

The deputy nodded. "The trailer, too. Maybe your friend left when they evacuated the island."

"Not unless he walked out of here. What about the boat?"

"I haven't seen a boat."

Erik figured as much and took a few uneasy steps toward the sea. The fact that Samuelson's Airstream and boat trailer were still parked on the island left him with a troubling account of what had likely taken place.

If Samuelson had been notified of the approaching storm, he would have moved to higher ground. It was obvious to Erik that his friend hadn't received a warning. Two other questions haunted him. Who else had visited the trailer, and where were Samuelson's journals and core samples?

He joined the deputy beside his patrol vehicle. "I think Samuelson may have been out to sea when the storm hit. You'd better notify the Coast Guard. Tell them to commence a search and to be on the lookout for a twenty-foot Whaler."

The deputy stared dumbly ahead.

"What are you waiting for?" Erik said, snapping his fingers. "Get on it!"

Erik returned to the trailer with an empty box and retrieved what he could. After stowing the box in the Suburban, he drove out to the edge of the muddy sea where an endless string of breakers crashed on shore.

The gray horizon stretched out before him, devoid of ships or boats or any sign of his friend. Sloppy seas bucked in the wake of the storm, like the telltale exhaust from a mighty machine.

A ferocious hurricane by the time she made landfall, Arlene had initially spun to life as a listless eddy spawned by the Coriollis effect of the Earth's rotation, a whirlwind dancing off the Sahara.

Energized over tropical seas, the storm had forged itself into a deadly atmospheric engine—a tightly packed storm capable of unleashing so much latent energy that the combined arsenals of the world's superpowers would have had trouble keeping her in rotation for a single day.

Brian watched a breaking wave roar down the beach. He recalled the day Samuelson purchased the twenty-foot Whaler and felt an emptiness in his chest. The boat had been his pride and joy, but surviving a Category 3 hurricane required more than steadfast seamanship and an unsinkable hull. Successfully navigating a hurricane would have required a miracle.

CHAPTER 13

Requiem

The sun slipped from the horizon with imperceptible slowness. Erik stared out at the tortured sea—he'd had a bad feeling about the storm from the start. Perhaps if he had stayed at the Hurricane Center things would have worked out differently. He might have seen something the Doppler radar had missed or sensed something the others hadn't. And maybe he would have succeeded in warning his friend.

Realizing he'd be late returning to Augusta, he punched the hotel number into his cell phone and waited to be put through to Tai.

As Hunting Island faded from sight, a feeling of unease overcame him, memories of a stealthy wave prowling the night, something large and looming and ready to swallow him up.

His cell phone came to life, and he snatched it to his ear.

Tai said, "Did you find Samuelson?"

"I think he got into big trouble out here."

"What sort of trouble?"

"I found his trailer and pickup, but his boat's missing and the surf's breaking huge along the beach—it doesn't look good."

"What are you going to do?"

"I've done all I can. I notified the authorities and told them to radio the Coast Guard."

"Do you think he was out to sea when Arlene came ashore?"

"It's beginning to look that way. Something must've happened aboard his boat." Erik was quiet for a moment. "Solar activity's been doing a number on communications, maybe his radio went out."

"I'm afraid I've got more bad news," she said. "Deevers called a mandatory meeting for noon tomorrow, probably wants to fill us in on the latest from Washington. Anyway, I scheduled us aboard a return flight, first thing tomorrow morning."

"Just as well," he said. "There's nothing more I can do out here, not without a boat."

Back at the Hurricane Center, news of Samuelson's disappearance spread. Small groups gathered in the halls and behind closed doors, hazarding guesses about his whereabouts. Some of the staff held out hope, while others awaited final irrefutable word of his death. Day after day, hope eroded, slowly giving way to despair.

On the eighth day following his return from Savannah, Erik received a voicemail message from the Seventh Coast Guard District's Operations' Division.

He secured an outside line and rang the call back number. After several transfers, he advanced up the telephonic chain of command until connected with the appropriate party.

"Montoya here," said the voice. "What can I do for you?"

"This is Erik Reynard, with the National Hurricane Center in Miami. You have some news about a missing boat?"

"With two-million square miles of ocean to patrol, the Seventh District stays pretty busy. Every once in a while, we manage to find what we're looking for, like deserted boats left adrift."

Erik fell backwards and stared at the ceiling. What did he mean, deserted?

"A Reliance Class Cutter out of Base Charleston spotted your boat. Partially submerged, it posed a navigational hazard. It's a good thing we found it. Anyway, they off-loaded the vessel over on Hilton Head and left it with the local sheriff, turns out the boat was registered to a Jon Samuelson."

"Did they...?" Erik said, trying to put the right words together. "I mean, were there...?"

"Survivors? No sign of anyone on or anywhere near the subject vessel. The boat was found about thirty miles from shore, she'd taken quite a battering. A couple of rescue swimmers had to struggle through heavy seas to rig the boat for hoisting. This fellow, Samuelson, I take it he was a friend of yours?"

Erik managed a feeble, "Yes."

"Sorry, I wish I had better news."

Erik had heard all he needed to and cradled the receiver. Shuffling down the corridor leading to the director's office, he imagined Samuelson behind his desk, just like old times, as if nothing had happened. The sight of Deevers with his back to the door and the phone pinned against his greasy ear pretty much killed that image.

Shortly after he had accepted the assignment to preside over the National Hurricane Center, Deevers had the director's office enlarged, making it the most spacious office at the center.

The door was open. Inside, the walls were covered with commendations, professional citations and pictures of the director enjoying the sporting life with a host of influential Washington power brokers.

Erik stepped closer, his gaze slowly sweeping the room. In one photograph, Deevers shared a golf cart with Senator Crockett. In another, he drove golf balls with the Deputy Secretary of Commerce. Nearby, another photograph showed Deevers attempting a difficult putt while the Under Secretary For Oceans and Atmosphere watched from the edge of the green. Beneath the photograph was a small plaque mentioning something about gratitude. A three-by-five picture beside it revealed a younger, more hirsute Deevers seated behind a large desk at a little known information gathering agency in Wallops, Virginia.

Deevers left nothing to chance. As a marginally competent scientist, every career move he had made was politically engineered to yield the most lucrative advancement possible.

Erik tapped on the glass with his ring.

Deevers swung around and motioned him inside. He directed Erik toward a chair and wrapped up his call.

"If this has something to do with Samuelson's boat, I've

already heard. The Commander of the Seventh Coast Guard District's an old friend of mine."

Who wasn't? Erik thought.

"He's the one who tipped me off," Deevers said, watering a prickly desk cactus with the last of his coffee. "We met during my stint at the Pentagon. Samuelson's name still carries plenty of weight. They knew who they were searching for."

Erik soon got over the fact that he'd been privileged to second-hand information at best, details the director already knew.

Deevers cleaned beneath his thumbnail with a chrome letter opener. "Look, Samuelson was a bright guy, and he's going to be missed. But don't make life any tougher than it is."

"What are you trying to say?"

"Do I have to spell it out? How long do you think an exposed man could survive out there? How long has it been, a week? More?"

He tapped the chrome letter opener against his palm and leveled it in Erik's direction. "A few years from now, I'll be out of here. Retired and collecting my pension. Playing golf and enjoying pool-side pina coladas. Who knows? By then, maybe you'll be running this place. In the meantime, do yourself a favor—be a team player."

"Samuelson was my friend, and I let him down. I should have seen the hurricane coming."

"You were in Houston, remember?"

"That's right," Erik said with an angry stare. "I was."

"Accidents happen," Deevers said. "Systems occasionally break down."

"Who'll continue his work?"

"No one here, I assure you. The World Weather Conference wasn't ready to hear what he had to say twenty years ago, and it's unlikely anyone's ready for his exaggerated theories now. Besides, look where it got him—divorced and missing at sea. That's a hell of a legacy to leave behind."

"A hundred years from now, Samuelson will be credited for his findings, for raising people's consciousness, about the weather, the environment—all of it."

Deevers' face flushed an interesting shade of red. "His assertions are provocative and unproven. In my opinion, they're dangerous. All they'd do is create panic, and people are uptight enough about the weather."

Erik remained silent.

"The drought-induced rise in food prices already has the Department of Agriculture pretty freaked out," Deevers said. "Frankly, I don't want to hear that my people are fanning the flames of hysteria."

"Put your head in the sand if you want to, but that won't alter the facts. Like it or not, the weather's changing." Erik turned toward a blackboard and sketched a hurricane with a squeaky piece of chalk. "Not three-hundred miles across, but a thousand maybe fifteen-hundred miles across. We're talking monster storms here."

Deevers listened.

"What would you say if I told you we're likely to see storms packing sustained winds of two-hundred-miles-per-hour, maybe two-fifty?"

"I've warned you for the last time, keep those wild notions to yourself."

"Is that all?" Erik said.

"Not quite. The authorities out on Hunting Island claim Samuelson's trailer was picked clean. Don't suppose you know anything about that?"

"Somebody from the Department of Weather got there before I did. Maybe you should speak with them."

"I didn't order anyone up there."

A long pause followed, and neither man blinked.

"If Samuelson's research is as misdirected as you say, why are you so interested?"

"People want to know what he was up to, people near the top. In case you haven't noticed, the weather's a matter of national security."

Erik stared silently out the window.

"Look, Erik, you're the best hurricane specialist I've got. Soon, the Department of Weather will have more funding than ever and less red tape. We can vastly improve weather prediction, and you figure prominently in the future of this center. But if you keep alarming people with talk of violent weather, you'll have to answer to me." Deevers made a jabbing gesture with the letter opener. "No surprises, understand? You have something to say, come see me first."

Erik shook his head. "In 1952 a black fog rolled silently into London. Officials had been warned about elevated levels of sulfur dioxide due to the city's reliance on coal, but chose to ignore it. When the fog cleared, more than four thousand people were dead."

"What's your point?"

"Destructive forces are aligning, and the public has a right to know."

"If you want to be a catastrophe modeler, I suggest you sign on with an insurance company."

"I'm a hurricane specialist."

"Then do your job, damn it! Better yet, I'm sending you over to Public Affairs for awhile. It might do you some good. You can help plan field trips, predict raincoat weather, that sort of thing."

Public Affairs did much more than plan field trips, and everyone knew it. Everyone, it seemed, but Deevers.

"You're demoting me?"

"Let's call it a temporary transfer."

"What about forecasting?"

"Consider yourself reassigned."

"For how long?"

"Until you're willing to play along."

Without saying a word, Erik stormed through the doorway and down the hall.

CHAPTER 14

Ocean Broadcasting Headquarters
New York City

Robert Ocean exited a private elevator outside the penthouse suite of his Park Avenue office, the Eagle's Nest as he was fond of calling it. His adversaries had a different name for the place: Viper Den.

A middle-aged woman looked up from behind a formidable desk and rose to greet him. "Good morning, Mr. Ocean," she said in a heavy brogue. "Mr. Spicer's waiting for you inside."

He mumbled something without looking up and strolled across the marble foyer.

Just outside his office was a sterling serving tray—a single rose, coffee, a newspaper and a fresh-off-the-press copy of Ocean Broadcasting's annual report. He lifted the report and smiled at his profile, prominently displayed on the cover. Beneath his portrait were written the words *Information is Power*.

His secretary looked on adoringly. "It's a wonderful likeness."

"It is at that."

He admired his reflection in the glass door leading to his inner sanctum on which was etched a cresting sea wave, the company's corporate seal.

The door opened automatically upon his approach. Once inside, he smoothed his silk tie and commanded the shutters to open. A moment later, sunlight beamed across the room and he heard the sound of hollow clapping.

"Bravo!" came a familiar voice.

A match flared, and a man in the shadows puffed a cigar to life. Shafts of sunlight blazed through the smoke, a hint of leather with an earthy finish.

Ocean inhaled deeply through his nose. "I see you found the Montecristos."

"You, sir, have a highly developed sense of smell."

"It helps me discern bullshit. Help yourself to a Diplomatico, counselor, they're right next to the Montecristos," Ocean said, nodding toward the humidor. "You apparently know the way."

"I thought Cubans were illegal?"

"Haven't you heard? I'm the Weather Czar—I can have whatever I want."

"Of course."

Ocean turned toward the zebra skin couch, and his smile grew teeth. "Did you know it takes longer to learn how to make a fine cigar than it does to make partner in that paper mill you call a law firm?"

"Be nice, Robert. I just came by to congratulate you. You must tell me, how did the appointment come about?"

"Simple. During the campaign, we made certain the President received the best possible coverage. We had our cameras rolling at every possible photo op—kissing babies, promising inner city aid, that sort of thing."

"Sounds expensive."

"A worthwhile investment," Ocean said. "Some creative re-shaping by the press and voila! The President is once again America's favorite son."

"And to the victor go the spoils."

"Something like that. Anyway, I received a personal thank you from his highness on election night. When he asked how he could return the favor, I assured him we'd think of something."

"Like overseeing the newly created Department of Weather?"

"Can you think of anyone more deserving?"

Spicer appeared contemplative, and Ocean pitched him a copy of the company's latest annual report.

"*Information is Power*, it's our new corporate credo."

Spicer examined the cover, lingering on each syllable.

"Throughout history, those in power have occupied the high ground," Ocean said. "Today, the high ground orbits the earth—satellites, my dear Spicer, our eyes in the sky."

"I see."

"Not everyone has the luxury of being born to an Ivy League legacy. This company's success is the result of a lifetime of hard work and determination. I have a destiny to fulfill," Ocean said, getting in Spicer's face. "Do you have any goals, Karl?"

The attorney nodded halfheartedly.

"A person without goals is pre-wired for failure, their life's work nothing but one sad disappointment after another."

"I couldn't agree more."

"Of course, fulfilling one's destiny occasionally means engaging in activities some might consider controversial."

"Like influencing politicians?"

"Precisely."

Spicer drew heavily on his cigar, momentarily disappearing behind a cloud of smoke.

Ocean turned toward an ornate birdcage. "Those in positions of power must do what's in their best interest."

"You can count on me," Spicer said, studying the animal mounts adorning the room. "We're on the same team, Robert. What's good for Ocean Broadcasting is good for the firm."

"You're such a politician," Ocean said with a sigh. "At least you're my politician."

Ocean clucked at a pair of lovebirds flitting about the cage and worked his hand inside. One of the small birds lit on his finger.

"I trust your firm will be able to handle the work?"

"We'll have no problem serving your legal needs, you have my word."

"I'm glad to hear that."

Spicer twisted the tail of a stuffed lion, frozen in an aggressive leap.

"You can only twist a lion's tail so far," Ocean said. "Come to him with a scrap of horse meat or a bloody knee joint and he'll purr like a kitten. Run out of meat and, well, you know..."

The attorney shifted nervously in his seat.

"So tell me, Karl, what have you brought for me today, a scrap of horse meat or a bloody knee joint?"

Spicer inched toward the window and stared down five-hundred feet into the street below. "Globalcom's board rejected your offer. If we persist with a greenmail campaign to turn the shareholders' vote, they're threatening a poison pill."

Ocean's hand tightened into a fist, and the small bird darted for the safety of the cage wall.

"Poison pill? Tell me, who are they planning to acquire?"

"Some satellite leasing company," Spicer said, downing a shot of brandy. "A real dog, knee high in debt. Lost a high-tech bird when a rocket blew last month. Zapel over in Mergers and Acquisitions tells me they won't see their way into the black for five years, minimum. Beyond that, who knows? Actually, it could work out to be a strategic move on Globalcom's part in the long run, providing they sell their shareholders on the idea."

"I don't need more satellites," Ocean said, latching the cage door. "Soon I'll have access to the best in the world, care of a little known agency called NESDIS."

Ocean quickly reconsidered his offer to acquire a controlling interest in Globalcom. The bloom, as they say, was definitely off the rose.

"Screw it! Dump the shares tomorrow. See if our traders can arrange some sales prior to the opening. We'll still walk away with a profit. I only wish I could short the damn stock."

"Are you sure you want to liquidate?"

"Like my daddy used to say, if you can't buy the horse, you might as well cripple it."

Just then, he noticed his secretary standing outside the door and motioned her to enter.

"What is it, Ms. Donovan?"

"Sorry, sir, but it's Sister Michaels. She called to remind you about the groundbreaking ceremony for the new hospital wing. It's planned for noon tomorrow."

"Tell her I'll be there."

His secretary chanced a smile. "It's a wonderful thing you've done. My sister was treated at that hospital."

Spicer used the opportunity to make his way back inside

the humidor for a handful of Cubans.

Keeping a cautious eye on him, Ocean said, "Have they arranged delivery of my bust?"

"It arrives this afternoon," she said, "kept covered, of course, right up until the groundbreaking ceremony."

"Hear that, Karl? I'm being memorialized."

The attorney closed the door to the humidor and raised his brandy. "Here's to charitable remainder trusts."

"That'll be all," Ocean said, dispatching the woman. "Hold my calls."

Once the glass door closed behind her, Ocean looked back at his guest. "So what do you suppose that charitable gift saved me?"

"Millions."

"Perhaps I'll keep you around, you're already saving me money. Have you met Gustav Bruner?"

"Afraid I haven't had the pleasure."

"He's joining us from a security firm headquartered in Johannesburg. He's been working with the Communications Group in South Carolina, and arrives this evening at Kennedy. I'd like you to be there to meet him...break the ice, as they say."

"Background investigations?"

Ocean nodded and considered the world beyond his window. "I had an enlightened discussion with officials from the National Weather Service about satellites. They approved a tie-in with Ocean Broadcasting in an attempt to improve weather prediction, an unprecedented alliance between business and government. The President's even given his blessing. I'm sending Bruner down to Virginia to work out the details."

Spicer drew heavily on his cigar. A moment later, gray smoke streamed from between his lips.

"One of my first duties as Weather Secretary will be to oversee the design and construction of our new headquarters. When the design work goes out for bid, I want my nephew's firm to get the contract."

"Is it minority owned?" Spicer asked.

"No."

"A woman-owned business, perhaps?"

"I'm afraid not," Ocean said, losing patience.

"With the way government contracts are being awarded these days..."

"Spicer?"

"Yes, sir?"

"I pay your firm far too much to hear a bunch of excuses. Now then, the name of the design firm is Dern, Kilpatrick and Greene. I don't care who bids on the job, but when the contract is awarded, I expect it to be to them. Is that clear?"

Spicer stuffed the Cubans into his coat pocket. "Quite clear."

Chapter 15

Reunion

When Michael Simms discovered Professor Yoshida would be serving as a short-term advisor at the National Hurricane Center, he couldn't resist inviting himself along. He didn't need much of a reason to see Tai. Besides, the plane ride and bag of salted peanuts were free.

Yoshida's inaugural flight with the Hurricane Hunters had been an initiation of sorts. And to Michael's surprise, Yoshida welcomed his company.

After touching down in Miami, Michael picked up a rental car and shuttled them over to the Hurricane Center where Erik met them just inside the entrance.

Erik raised his hand to receive a high-five. "Well, if it isn't the Hurricane Hunter."

"Bonjour, Doc. Hope you've been taking care of my baby."

Tai strolled down the hall and smiled. "I can take care of myself, thanks."

"There you go," said Erik.

Yoshida peered above the rim of his glasses, pulling his earlobe as he listened.

Michael said, "By the way, this is Dr. Yoshida. We shared a flight into Miami."

Half bowing, Yoshida stretched his hand toward Erik, then Tai. "It's a pleasure meeting both of you."

"We met once before," Erik said, returning the handshake, "in

Boston. You were a visiting lecturer."

"Welcome to the National Hurricane Center," Tai added cheerfully. "I know of your work."

"So I heard. Colonel Simms told me all about you."

"You don't say?" she said, shooting a promising wink Michael's way.

After they got beyond the formalities, Yoshida inquired about Dr. Samuelson. Tai and Erik looked at each other, neither one speaking for a time.

Erik said, "I'm afraid there's been an accident. Samuelson left the Hurricane Center a couple of months ago, right after the big shakeup. He'd been doing independent field research along the eastern seaboard—paleoclimatological work."

"What happened?"

"He was out to sea when the hurricane made landfall. I'm afraid he never got a storm warning, nobody did. Sunspots fried our communications, and nothing but static left NESDIS all night."

"I had nothing but respect for Jon, ever since I heard him address the U.N., nearly twenty years ago."

"His theory on hurricanes and global warming?" Erik said.

"Precisely."

The fact that Yoshida was so familiar with Samuelson and his work fascinated Erik. The two men had obviously known each other pretty well.

"We were both staying at the same hotel while attending the conference. One evening, we bumped into each other in the lounge and had the opportunity to talk weather at length. Who's the center's new director?"

"That would be me," Deevers said, stepping through the doorway. "Welcome to the National Hurricane Center, Professor. I'm sure Reynard, here, will be only too happy to help you get situated. You can share his office."

"Thank you."

Erik was about to protest sharing his office when he felt a bump from Tai's shoulder.

"Be nice," she whispered.

Erik feigned an obligatory smile. What was he supposed to do, act as if nothing had happened? Pretend he hadn't been taken off hurricane watch?

Deevers gave Michael the once over. "And you would be?"

"Colonel Simms, sir—weather recon out of Keesler."

"You're one of Red York's men."

"That's right."

Deevers glanced over at Tai. "Why don't you give the Colonel a tour?"

"I'd love to," she said, offering the crook of her arm.

As Michael and Tai disappeared down the corridor, Yoshida said to Erik, "I can't believe Samuelson's gone, his passing is a tragic loss."

"The Coast Guard called a week ago, they located his capsized boat. I never thought it would come to this." Erik hesitated for a moment before changing the subject. "Let me show you around."

Yoshida followed him down the hallway leading to his office and paused briefly outside the door. "Did you say Samuelson had been studying core samples taken along the Barrier Islands?"

"That's right."

"Did he happen to mention Christmas Island? Anything about samples taken from prehistoric reefs?"

Erik nodded. "Something about low strontium levels in ancient corals."

"I'd hoped to meet with him, to compare notes."

"When Samuelson ran the Center, he encouraged free-thinking research. It's not the same these days. I've been warned to keep my wild theories to myself."

"Sounds like he was more than just a boss."

For an instant Erik felt outside himself, as if Samuelson were suddenly very near, as if time had stopped and rewound. He felt like he'd had the same discussion with Yoshida a hundred times before.

"More like a father," Erik said at last, shaking off the rapture of deja vu.

"The change will begin with the jet stream," Yoshida said, "a divine wind." He rotated his head as if searching for eavesdroppers and nudged the office door shut. "The weather is changing, but one of Samuelson's critical assumptions may have been wrong. The super-storms he expected may be stronger than anticipated."

"How strong?"

"Who do I look like, the guy from the evening weather forecast?"

Erik smiled for the first time in a week. Yoshida began to laugh, ever so slowly at first. He resembled one of those carved Hotei figures sold in gift shops, the ones with the round bellies and mirthful grins. His laugh was contagious, and Erik soon found himself joining in.

Yoshida glanced at something atop Erik's desk. "Man Fighting The Tide," he remarked, lifting the small stone archer.

"How'd you know that?"

"Two trips across the South China Sea. Did you know an emperor once sent ten thousand archers to stop the mighty Qiantang during flood tide? The river swallowed their arrows and overflowed its bank." Yoshida lowered the artifact. "The Black Dragon swept thousands to their deaths during the eighteenth century and killed another eighty-seven people back in '93."

Erik studied the small stone archer guarding the corner of his desk, bow raised in service to his emperor. He could almost hear the sound of Samuelson's voice. His friend was surely gone, and Erik himself was off hurricane watch, indefinitely.

He polished a framed photograph of Samuelson with the heel of his hand. Two other pictures occupied the wall above his desk—a satellite photograph of Guam in the aftermath of super typhoon Omar and a stretch of flooded wasteland near Bangladesh.

Yoshida shuffled toward the second photograph. "I know this place, the Bay of Bengal."

"A tropical cyclone down there recently took out a drilling rig and everyone aboard," Erik said.

Yoshida shook his head. "Twenty brave men and women. Such a waste of human life."

"If I didn't know better, I would have guessed you were there."

"Briefly, as a consultant. I tried to warn them. In 1970, a cyclone in the bay killed close to a million. Only once before have I seen destruction on such a scale."

"Want to know what I call killer storms?" Erik said. "I call them monsters."

CHAPTER 16

Knock-knock

Erik was belting out his best aria when the knocking started. He spun the squeaky shower faucet to off, cinched a towel around his waist and bolted down the hall toward the door. The knocking grew louder by the second.

"Just a second," he said, gripping the doorknob with one hand and the knotted towel in the other.

Nothing could have prepared him for what he saw next—Heather Conroy leaning against the railing outside his apartment, backlit in the haze of a neon sign advertising a neighborhood Szechwan joint. She did absolute wonders for the jeans and cashmere sweater she wore. In her arms she carried a grocery bag, overflowing with goodies.

She shifted the bag in her arms. "How long does a girl have to knock?"

"Sorry, I was in the shower. Sometimes with the water on full and the tile, well, you can barely hear yourself think."

"Really?" she said. "I could hear you singing clear out in the parking lot. Puccini?"

"Francesco Cilea—was I any good?"

"Not bad."

Realizing he was half-naked, he ducked back behind the door and retied his towel.

"Is that your car out front?" she asked.

"Which one?"

"The little red coupe they're towing."

Erik rushed past her and hollered, "Come on, give me a break."

He was too late. The tow truck driver either didn't hear him or refused to, and he watched his car disappear down the road. He stood there for a moment, seething in silence. Ten minutes in the damn tow-away zone, talk about heartless.

"It could use a paint job," she said.

"Cut me some slack, they just impounded my damn car."

"What is it, anyway?"

"It's a Saab," he said. "They're Swedish."

"What's with the license plate, 74 MPH?"

"It's a weather thing, the wind speed at which tropical storms become hurricanes."

"That's cute," she said.

Combing his hair into place with his fingers, he smiled and tried to forget about his car. His unexpected guest was far more interesting.

"So, are you going to invite me in, or shall we stand out here all night?"

He nearly tripped over himself as he swung the door open wide. She gave his bachelor pad a quick three-sixty, letting her eyes linger on a rowing machine, an overflowing desk and a coagulating lava lamp.

"What do you call it, new millennium minimalist?"

"I'm between decorators."

"It could use a woman's touch."

As far as Erik was concerned, she had the job. He inhaled the scent of fine perfume as she sauntered past.

Inside the grocery bag he spotted a bottle of Stolichnaya Cristall, a tin of Caspian Sea caviar and a fancy-looking box of gourmet crackers.

"What's the occasion?" he said.

"No occasion. I remembered you were partial to vodka and thought you might enjoy a little company."

"Vodka's fine, I'm not driving. Not tonight, anyway."

"Where'd you acquire a taste for vodka?"

"Down in the Antarctic. About ten years ago, after I left MIT."

Heather moved past the living room and easily found the kitchen. Erik used the opportunity to dash down the hallway. He slid into a pair of jeans and pulled on a faded college sweatshirt. "It gets pretty cold down there. I've learned to appreciate warmer climes."

"Was a woman involved?"

"You're full of questions."

"Sorry, but the Antarctic seems so extreme. The sort of desolate, edge-of-the-earth destination that draws lovelorn scientists, like French legionnaires and the Sahara. All that ice, it's practically a metaphor for loneliness."

Recalling the frozen landscape he'd once called home, Erik said, "There was this young Latvian scientist named Masha."

"I can't wait for the details."

He smiled with the memory as he strolled into the living room. Beyond the tile counter, a halogen spotlight shone down on her like a star.

Pulling his hair back into a ponytail, he plopped onto the sofa and began to reminisce. "Masha Zeberina, she used to serenade me on a busted Cuban guitar, singing American folk songs while the persistent Antarctic sun tried to set. Old John Denver, that sort of thing. Anyway, she reached the end of her tour before I did and left aboard the Russian ice breaker, Sibir." He sniffed once and raised an empty glass. "She broke my frozen heart."

"Poor thing," she said, burying her head in the refrigerator. "What can I do to make it better?"

He lowered the light of a nearby table lamp. "We'll think of something."

Heather withdrew a bottle of mixer from the fridge and arranged it along with the Stolichnaya, a mismatched pair of glasses, gourmet crackers and caviar on a cutting board turned serving tray.

She wadded the plastic bag into a can beneath the sink and rose a moment later with an unopened letter in hand. "Who's Claudette Theriault? Another old flame?"

"Why do you ask?" he said, feeling like he'd downed a jigger of battery acid.

"Because there's an unopened letter from her in the trash. Here, I'll bring it to you."

Heather clicked on the light he'd just subdued and handed him the unopened letter. Erik tapped it against his palm.

"Never misses a birthday." With the spark of the moment growing dim, he added, "She's my mother."

"What was the letter doing in the trash?"

"How many days are you planning on staying?"

"Long story, huh?"

"She wouldn't recognize me if we shared a cab."

"You never mentioned having a mother."

"Neither did you."

"Very tricky," she said. "I'll ask the questions around here."

"Everyone's from somewhere," he said, "unless you send Mother's Day cards to a test tube. She packed her bags and left during a storm. My father chased after her and lost control of his truck, plowed into a flooded ditch. Dead. My grandparents took me in, they raised me. What else do you want to talk about?"

"I guess the subject of you and your mother is off limits."

"Afraid so," he said, measuring a tall shot of Stoly into a glass.

"So, what's new at the Hurricane Center?"

The vodka went down like hot ice. "Deevers yanked me out of forecasting and assigned me to Public Affairs. I think he's got it in for me."

"I thought you were the most qualified forecaster at the Center."

"Specialist," he corrected, clinking his glass against hers.

"Right...specialist. Anyway, I can't believe he demoted you."

"Let's call it a temporary transfer, shall we? Fact is, Deevers is worried about making a big splash with the new Weather Czar. He doesn't want me to say anything too provocative."

"Any chance you can get me an interview with Ocean Broadcasting?"

"You're not using me, are you?"

Heather turned up her hundred-watt smile. "Perish the thought."

"I'm not the only one concerned with changing weather

cycles. We've got a visiting professor from Texas Tech down at the center, maybe you should talk to him, name's Yoshida. I can't believe the guy's still at it, must be eighty years old."

Heather moved effortlessly across the room, balancing a caviar-laden cracker on the fingertips of one hand and her cocktail in the other. She stopped near the doorway outside a spare bedroom.

"What are you building?"

"It's nothing," he said, coaxing her back toward the living room. "Did I mention NOAA's Geophysical Fluid Dynamics Laboratory at Princeton? They're doing some interesting stuff with numeric modeling."

The words were lost on Heather, and she clicked on the light for a better look. She crouched to view an architectural model at eye level. A half-dozen skyscrapers rose from a cityscape, and she reached down to lift the one closest to her.

"What's with these models?"

"Careful," he said, removing it from her grip. "They're fragile."

He lowered the building onto the cityscape and rotated the structure several degrees.

"Fragile, are they?" she chided, plunking her wet glass down on the miniature boulevard.

He lifted her drink and blotted the smudge. "Yes they are. And if you must know, it's a cityscape."

"Lighten up."

Concerned that he may have hurt her feelings, he switched out of weather nerd mode. They were models for God's sake—balsa wood, cardboard and glue. What was a few hundred hours of work?

"Sorry, I guess I overreacted."

"You're forgiven. What city is this, anyway? It doesn't resemble any place I've ever seen."

"It's an amalgamation, different coastal urban centers. For instance, this building," he said, pointing to the skyscraper she'd just put down, "is Central Plaza, Hong Kong, seventy-eight stories and over twelve hundred feet. Over there's Texas Commerce Tower in Houston at just over a thousand feet."

"What about that one?"

"That's First Interstate's World Center in Los Angeles, one thousand eighteen feet."

"What's the significance?"

"I'm conducting a wind load study. These models represent the world's tallest buildings—each within the potential striking distance of hurricanes."

He swept his hand slowly across the model, knocking the models onto their sides. "Not a pretty picture, I'm afraid."

"Storms that destroy entire cities?" she said. "Come on."

"Theoretically, it's possible. Wind speed's only half the problem. Storm tide and rain-driven flooding are the real killers. Back in 1900, eight thousand people died in Galveston when a storm surge inundated the island. In human terms, it was the costliest natural disaster in American history."

"That's awful."

"What are you gonna do?" he said. "Insurance companies keep insuring against the risk, banks keep lending and contractors keep building, right up to the ocean's edge. When the big one comes, and it will come, the destruction will be devastating. I don't even want to think about what would happen if New Orleans took a direct hit from a monster storm, or New York for that matter. We try to get our warnings out in time, but prediction's an imperfect science."

"Is this how you spend your spare time," she said, "dreaming up disaster scenarios?"

"Sometimes I follow young women I barely know up to their hotel rooms. I practically have to fight off the storm groupies."

"You don't say," she whispered, wrapping her arms around his neck. "Care for another drink?"

"Not on your life. Tonight's a night I plan to remember."

"*Waiting for the big blow?*"

"In a matter of speaking." He smiled and led her back toward the living room. "I have a collection of hurricane recordings if you're interested."

Heather dimmed the lights. "Never know, you might get lucky."

CHAPTER 17

Some like it hot

Erik stared across the hood of his Saab at curbside, reading an upside down message written in the dust. *Wash me.*

Showers had been expected for days, and he'd held out as long as he could. It wouldn't do to wash his car the day before it rained. It sort of blew the forecaster image.

Tai and Michael were running late. They'd arranged to meet at the corner barbecue joint at a quarter past twelve, and it was now twelve-thirty.

Erik joined a half-dozen patrons gathered beneath a red, white and green awning. Barbecue smoke billowed from a rooftop stovepipe like the chimney of a snowbound cabin.

A pretty, full-figured woman greeted him warmly, caramel complexion, hair tightly curled and shiny black. Most noticeable were her nails, bubble gum pink and a good two inches long.

"Just one today?" she asked, fanning her face with an order pad.

"I'm waiting for some friends, three of us in all."

She leaned close enough for him to smell her perfume and whispered, "That nice window seat up front will be available in five."

He gave the restaurant the proverbial once-over. At the rear of the joint, a noisy fan cleaved the air, drawing heat from the kitchen. The hostess returned and showed him to his table.

Tai appeared in the doorway a few minutes later, mouthing

the word, "Sorry."

Erik stood. "No sweat, I just got here myself."

"I hope you're hungry," she said, reaching the table with Michael in tow.

"Starved."

The waitress sashayed over with menus, settings for three and a special smile for Erik and Michael.

"Ready when you are," she said cheerfully.

Michael turned to Erik and whispered, "I think she's sweet on you. A woman like that can..."

Before he could finish, Tai shot an elbow into his side.

"What's wrong with you, baby? I think you broke a rib."

"A woman like that can what?"

"What woman?" he whispered, draping his arm around her shoulder and kissing her cheek.

"Hmm, I think I'd better keep a closer eye on you."

"Help yourself to some peanuts," said the waitress. "You can toss the shells on the floor."

Erik thought about Heather and tossed a handful of empty shells with impunity—it had been quite a while since he'd seen her. The nuts were fresh and salty, but they were a poor substitute for his girl.

The brick red floor was covered with sawdust and peanut shells, and the food was served in green plastic baskets lined with wax paper. Ribs, chicken, quartered deep-fried potatoes with the skin still on, sourdough rolls, hot-buttered corn on the cob and fat jalapenos—your typical heart attack on a plate.

The waitress slid behind Erik without him seeing. He knew she was there from the overwhelming wave of gardenia blossom. Standing close behind him, she placed a plastic bib around his neck and proceeded to tie it.

"There you go, baby," she said, sweetly.

Before she could squeeze into position behind Michael, Tai thrust her hand out to intercept the bib. "I'll take that."

"Suit yourself."

Tai slid behind Michael, pressing her body against his.

"What do we have here? A big, strappin', military man...a pilot even. I just love pilots."

The waitress watched from the other side of the restaurant,

arms folded defiantly over her substantial chest. She whispered something to the cook before going about her business.

Erik fussed with a bullet hole his finger found in the front plate window.

Tai turned to the passing waitress. "Excuse me?"

"Whatcha want?" said the woman, the sweet lilting voice gone.

"What's with the hole?"

The question seemed to perk her up a little. Resting a fist on the shelf of her hip, she swung in close and said, "Before my uncle bought the place, it was an I-talian restaurant. About fifteen years ago some big-time gangster was gunned down, right in that very spot. Fell face down in his linguini. Kind of a bad omen, so people quit coming around. Anyway, my uncle got the place for a song. Changed the sign and the food. The rest is history. It did-n't pay to replace the whole window for that bitty little hole."

The image of a chunk of sizzling brisket slathered with bar-becue sauce quickly lost its appeal, and Erik considered ordering something else.

"Do you have anything light, something without barbecue sauce?"

"How about a nice, honey-grilled chicken breast?"

"Perfect," he said, refolding the menu.

His friends ordered the luncheon special, hot and spicy.

"How's everything back at storm central?" Erik asked.

"Business as usual."

"I hope Yoshida's not getting too comfortable in my office."

"He's not angling for your job, if that's what you're worried about. Frankly, I think he's anxious to get back to the university."

"There's more to Yoshida than meets the eye," Erik said.

Michael nodded. "Amen."

"What do you mean?"

Erik wiped some empty peanut shells off the table. "Don't you know? He lost his wife and kid during the war...Hiroshima. He was in Osaka the day of the bombing."

"Why didn't you tell me?"

"You never asked," Erik said. "Now it's your turn, tell me something I don't know."

Tai hesitated for a moment. "The numbers are in from our offshore buoys. Sea temps have been rising pretty fast, especially in the Pacific."

"That's interesting."

"You don't seem too surprised," she said. "Maybe you know something I should know."

"Just a hunch."

"It's not nice to hold out."

"If Deevers wants my input, he knows where to find me. In the meantime, I'm giving guided tours of the center and keeping my mouth shut."

"When are you coming back? Everybody in Forecasting misses you."

"I was hoping you'd be able to tell me. Guess I'll have to take that up with Deevers."

Tai said, "If you ask me, it's beginning to look like the classic onset of an El Nino cycle."

"That's my baby," said Michael.

"Might be a blessing," Erik said. "El Nino could bring an end to the drought and offer some protection against Atlantic hurricanes."

Tai placed her napkin on her lap. "Careful what you wish for, the last El Nino hammered the west coast pretty hard."

The waitress arrived with a platter of lunch baskets balanced on her shoulder. Michael dug into a sizzling chunk of brisket while Tai went on about children, weddings and the prospect of setting up a home.

Michael began to sweat. He raised his napkin, but couldn't tamp the sweat from his forehead fast enough.

"All this talk of marriage making you nervous?" Erik said.

"No, man, it's this food!" He gulped down a full glass of tea. "It is h-o-t, hot."

Tai downed a bite and immediately reached for her tea as well. She drained the glass and begged for more.

The waitress walked over nice and easy with an icy pitcher of tea dressed up with a mint sprig.

"Food a little spicy? Guess the cook got carried away with the cayenne."

The fire wasn't anything the tea couldn't extinguish, and

Tai devoured her taters and corn.

Michael rose from the table. "I've gotta go, this tea's passing right through me."

"Don't get lost," Tai warned.

He let his hand trail over her shoulder as he slid behind her. "Don't worry, baby, I'll be right back."

Her eyes followed him all the way to the john, but she wasn't alone. The waitress was watching him, too. She glanced in Tai's direction and flashed a big peachy smile as if to register the indiscretion.

"Cow," Tai whispered, ventriloquist style.

"What are you worried about?" Erik said. "You're at least five years younger."

"And a good fifty pounds lighter."

"Still, she does have a certain appeal."

"You're hopeless," Tai said, keeping one eye fixed on the bathroom door. "So tell me, have you spoken to Heather?"

"She paid me a little visit."

"Mind if I give you some advice?"

Sensing he was going to receive her counsel whether he wanted it or not, he said, "It's a free country."

"I don't know if she's the best woman for you."

"What's that supposed to mean? Don't you think she could be attracted to someone like me?"

"That's not what I said."

"But that's what you're implying."

Tai took a deep breath. "It's just that...she seems superficial. Like she's got an agenda, and it involves you. And when you're together you drink too much."

"You're worse than my old grandmere."

"Somebody needs to keep an eye on you."

"So, I enjoy an occasional drink," he protested. "Maybe it's the only thing that quiets my mind. Do you have any idea what it's like to have the same nightmare, month after month, year after year?"

"Can't say I do, but people learn to deal with the past."

"What people?"

"My mother, for one. You're not the only person who's had to endure a little hardship in their life."

"Thanks for being so understanding. What's your mother's excuse?"

"Nightmares of Viet Nam and the war—summary executions, napalm, that sort of thing. She was lucky to make it out alive."

"How'd she escape?"

"She met my father, and he took her away from all that."

"What about the nightmares?"

"She still has them, but she copes. Maybe you should try it."

A nervous silence settled between them.

"Ever since Samuelson went missing, you've been drinking more and more. Face it, Erik, he's gone—and he isn't coming back."

He bit the inside of his cheek until it hurt and felt the stir of resentment. What he did in private was none of her damn business. Besides, Heather was the best thing that had ever happened to him.

"You've already been relegated to Public Affairs. Can't you see? It's affecting your job."

"That's where you're wrong," he shot back. "Coming forward with the truth is what's affecting my job. Something's being worked on us—systems are somehow being manipulated, the satellite blackouts, Samuelson being bounced out of the Hurricane Center and ending up missing at sea. Someone's behind this."

"Drinking doesn't help, and these groundless conspiracy theories..."

"Guess I know who my friends are," he said, rising to leave. "Thanks for lunch."

Chapter 18

Back in the saddle

Erik's eventual return to forecasting was met with fair weather. Congratulations, he told himself, just in time to celebrate the last half of the hurricane season. One thing was certain, Deevers was taking no chances.

Back in his office, Erik buried his head in a departmental bulletin and doodled a caricature of the fat-headed director in the margin.

During periods of relative calm, it was easy to become complacent, waiting for storms to manifest. Still, he knew better than to take the weather for granted.

Tai sneaked up and snapped the back of the bulletin with a flick of her finger. "Hey, stranger," she said, spinning into a nearby chair. "You still mad?"

He studied her for a few seconds without revealing the slightest emotion. "How could I stay mad at someone as sweet as you?"

"Did you hear the news?" she said. "Yoshida's extending his stay."

Erik disappeared behind the bulletin. "Is that a fact?"

"What are you reading?"

"About super typhoons, says here hot wire anemometers registered gusts over two hundred miles per hour during Typhoon Paka?"

"You don't say?" she said, adjusting a shiny clip in her hair.

"Sure you're not still mad?"

"I'll get over it."

"Truce?"

"You're not going to let me read, are you?"

The twinkle in her eyes said it all. He could read the darn bulletin any old time, any old time she wasn't around.

He lowered the bulletin to the table. "Apology accepted."

"Speaking of super typhoons, have you seen Heather lately?"

"No recent sightings in the greater Miami area."

"Sorry."

"I thought you didn't like her."

"Hey, I'm a woman. That was just my competitive side coming out. I guess I felt threatened."

"You, threatened? Come on, tell me it isn't so. I don't believe it."

"You really don't understand women, do you? See, I love Michael, and God willing we'll be married by this time next year. But you're my friend, and watching Heather cop that uppity attitude and the control she had over you, well, let's just say I didn't want you to lose your perspective or your pride."

Erik found himself nodding, as if he understood the mysterious ways of women. Nothing was farther from the truth.

Tai fussed with her hairclip. "So, I said to myself, honey, if she makes him happy, you should be happy for him. After all, I've already got my man."

She leaned forward and gave him a sisterly hug, then glanced down at the bulletin. "Did you see the rendering of the new headquarters in Washington?"

"Pretty hard to miss," Erik said, rotating the bulletin for a better look. "It's okay if you like neo-Nazi architecture. Says here they chose the same design team that did that monolithic regional mall outside Orlando, the one with the eight-story indoor ski slope. Ocean's nephew is a partner in the firm doing the design work."

Tai shrugged. "What's a little nepotism? By the way, Michael's due back next weekend. Why don't you join us for dinner?"

"I hate being a third wheel. Mind if I bring Heather

along?"

"Be my guest."

Truth was, he hadn't spoken to her for quite some time. He could always write, but first he'd have to find her address.

Their last date had gone well enough—they even spent part of the following day together. She joined him for breakfast, then gave him a lift to the impound yard where his vintage Saab awaited bail.

Erik recalled their farewell like it was yesterday, the way she'd blown him a kiss and smoked her tires. He remembered standing there, transfixed, staring at her taillights through the dust.

"Really hooked on her, aren't you?" Tai said, wresting him from the daydream.

"Does it show?"

"Just a little," she said with a wink.

CHAPTER 19

Unholy trinity

One could have mistaken the day Ocean and his entourage first visited the Hurricane Center for a presidential inauguration: windows squeaky clean, offices tidied up and Erik's six-foot stack of old newspapers gone.

The Weather Czar's jet-setting escapades made him irresistible to the press. Erik looked around at the fanfare and shook his head—irredeemable was more like it.

"He's not so bad," Tai said, "unless you think it's a sin to be wealthy."

"There's nothing wrong with money. It's just that he's under-qualified. He was a TV weatherman for God's sake."

Tai said, "An old college friend works for one of his newspapers. According to her, there's no glass ceiling. One year working for Ocean and she's zipping up the old editorial ladder."

Suddenly, everyone began to clap, and Erik found himself in the midst of a Bobby Ocean rally.

"He looks so distinguished," Tai said as he passed, "and taller than I thought."

"He's probably wearing lifts."

"Did you hear about the recent endowments he made in New York?"

"I read about it."

"If you ask me, corporate America ought to pay attention. Maybe his generosity will rub off."

"Are you blind?" Erik said. "The guy's all show. Those endowments and gifts are nothing but tax dodges. That's how the rich do it."

"Know what your problem is?" she said. "You're too damned cynical."

Erik mumbled something to himself and stared at the bulletin in his hands.

The Weather Czar reached the podium right on cue, his fashionably gray hair styled and his custom suit hanging wrinkle-free. He stood there with his jacket unbuttoned and his hands in his trouser pockets, the combined effect creating an aura of folksiness.

On his right he was flanked by Karl Spicer, Ocean Broadcasting's corporate counsel. To his left stood communications specialist Gustav Bruner. As captain of Ocean's transition team, the Aryan poster boy had been an outspoken advocate for the privatization of the weather service, an unpopular stance among the rank and file at NOAA.

Deevers was all smiles—less pasty, like he'd spent the previous day at a tanning salon, power tie over a crisp white shirt that fairly crackled.

"What's with him?" Erik said, loosening his ponytail from an elastic band.

"He never misses a photo op," Tai whispered through a clenched smile.

Employees streamed into the Media Room for a closer look at their celebrated boss. After a short introduction, including a list of Robert Ocean's many accomplishments with an emphasis on his charity work, Deevers vacated the podium.

A hearty round of applause followed, and Ocean cleared his throat to quiet the crowd. "Thank you. This state-of-the-art facility is without equal, and you," he said, motioning his arm about the room, "are among the world's finest weather professionals."

Tai whispered, "He must be talking about you."

Ocean leaned forward on the podium. "Uncertain times require extreme measures. With your help, we can restore the nation's confidence and put an end to the current crisis."

A spontaneous roar went up from the crowd. At long last,

the Department of Weather was coming into its own.

"We have a responsibility," he went on, eyes roving about the crowd, "to advance weather forecasting, assess climatic changes and promote safe navigation. Each and every one of you has a duty to uphold and an obligation to honor. We also have a proper image to convey."

Ocean leveled a serious stare at Erik, and he froze like a deer caught in high beams. After a few moments, the Weather Czar went on with his speech.

Erik wanted to disappear. "I'm screwed, the guy already hates me."

Much to Erik's dismay, Tai smiled approvingly at her new boss.

"Did you hear what I said?"

"Relax, it's nothing."

"How can you say that? He stared right at me while blathering on about image."

"Just wait until he recognizes your talent."

"Right, I'm sure Deevers will tell him all about it."

The expression on Tai's face summed-up Erik's worst fears. He should have concealed his long hair, maybe hidden his ponytail down the collar of his work shirt and worn a tie. A coat, perhaps. A button-down cotton shirt would have been better, something ivy, loafers and tweed, perhaps.

Instead, he wore his long hair freely down his back, looking like he'd dressed at a military surplus store and spent the night on a park bench.

A revelation came on quick as the Cajun two-step after a bowl of bad jambalaya. The culture of the National Weather Service was about to change in a very profound way.

Bobby Ocean's rah-rah speech ended with a rousing applause as the entire room rose to their feet. Deevers, power broker that he was, escorted the Weather Czar and assorted dignitaries out of the Media Room and back to his office, probably for an unofficial tête-à-tête.

Erik glanced over at Tai. She appeared incredibly awestruck, utterly and thoroughly enthralled. Perhaps he'd been too quick to judge.

"Still have misgivings?" she said.

"What the hell, I liked what he said about the Department of Weather's newly found autonomy."

"This is good. It's the first step toward overcoming your tendency toward antisocial behavior."

"Me?" he said. "Antisocial?"

Her observation began to sink in—maybe she was right. Perhaps it was the reason he'd had difficulty connecting with Heather, or anyone else for that matter.

"Nothing like being brutally honest," he said. "I feel like an incredible weight's been lifted. I almost feel like marching up the hall and giving old Deevers a hug."

"Don't get too carried away."

"I'll catch up with you tomorrow. It's going to be a wonderful day, nothing but blue skies."

Tai smiled and shook her head. "See you later, you nut."

CHAPTER 20

Censored

The moment Erik arrived at the Hurricane Center the following morning he realized something had gone terribly wrong.

He hastened down the hall, his previous forecast of blue skies quickly giving way to stormy weather. Associates, who ordinarily greeted him warmly, steered around him as if he were an outcast. What the hell was going on?

Once inside his office, he plunked into his chair and switched on the computer. Several minutes later he heard a familiar tapping against the glass.

"Door's open," he said.

Tai slipped inside and closed the door behind her, a folded newspaper beneath her arm.

"Grape?" he said, sliding a small plastic bag across the desk.

"No thanks," she said, shaking her head. "How long have you been back in forecasting?"

"About a week. Why?"

"You certainly know how to make a splashy entrance."

"Okay, I give up. I'm totally in the dark."

"I'll bet. What on Earth were you thinking, going public with that severe weather stuff? Or maybe I should be asking your girlfriend."

"Heather?"

Tai dropped the newspaper on his desk. "It's on the front

96

page, as if you didn't know."

He unfolded the morning news and focused on the headline: WAITING FOR THE BIG BLOW. Almost immediately, he spotted his own name peppered throughout the story.

"I never authorized this!" he complained, slapping the paper against his desk. "Who in the hell does she think she is?"

"Guess that's a question for your little friend."

"Deevers will need a defibrillator if he sees this."

"If?" she said, leaning against the door. "Better figure he's read it by now, honey. You're the talk of the town."

She gave him the sort of sad smile one reserves for the condemned, and excused herself.

A moment later, Deevers appeared outside his office, shoulders hunched like a vulture mantling road kill. Without uttering a sound, he motioned with a curled finger, beckoning Erik to follow. Not a single word was spoken until they reached the sanctity of the director's office with the door closed behind them.

Deevers paced, rolling the chrome letter opener deftly in his palm, eyes sharp as bits of flint, his face the unhealthy red of a cardiac patient.

"Really screwed the pooch this time," he said, driving the letter opener into his desk with a quiver. He whipped on a pair of reading glasses and snapped open the paper.

"I can explain," Erik said.

Deevers shushed him with an outstretched palm. "Monster storms imminent, says National Hurricane Center specialist, Dr. Erik Reynard." His eyes peered above the page, then descended once again beneath the headlines. "The weather is changing, warns Dr. Reynard, and people need to prepare, and so on, and so forth."

"I can explain."

"Don't talk," Deevers growled, "just listen. If it was up to me you'd be out on the street, understand?"

Erik nodded.

"I warned you to keep this crap to yourself, didn't I? You bet I did, damn it. I warned you."

Deevers circled the room, then stuck his finger in Erik's face like a weapon. He unrolled some antacids, tossed a few into his mouth and chewed them up in a hurry. Erik had never seen him so hot.

"Unfortunately, I can't fire you just because I feel like it. You're a federal employee, and I have to abide by collective bargaining agreements so I don't have the union all over my ass."

Erik remained standing while Deevers continued to vent. Finally, the letter opener came free of the desk.

"Pity you didn't commit an offense justifying summary dismissal," he said, waving the letter opener.

Each time Erik tried to speak in his own defense the director cut him off.

"Save it. Right now I don't want to hear anything you have to say." Deevers drummed his fingers on the desk. "God it pains me to do this."

"Do what?"

"I'm sending you on a little trip. The head of the Weather Service has been begging me to send someone out to California as part of an outreach effort, help them understand how we formulate forecasts, watches and warnings. Sort of a cultural exchange or sensitivity training—some kind of new-age crap the department dreamt up."

Realizing he had managed to duck the ax, Erik nodded.

"The Weather Service has four offices along the California coast, should take you about a week to visit them all. After that, well, let's just see what happens."

California sounded fine, especially knowing it killed Deevers to send him there. The director appeared to have one thing on his mind, arrange a temporary leave until an appropriate disciplinary action could be determined and meted out.

"Good day, Doctor."

Erik didn't know if he should clear out his office or not. After all, he hadn't been officially fired. Not yet, anyway.

CHAPTER 21

A tiger by the tail

Erik took his supper outside: three-alarm curry over Thai dirty rice, eaten right out of the takeout carton. Across the porch, a standoffish alley cat mewed at him hungrily.

"Hey, little meenoo—what's up?"

Erik watched the cat and wondered if he hadn't become just a little standoffish himself. He'd never gotten that close before.

"Looks like you could use a friend," he said, rising from his chair.

After pouring the cat some milk and himself a strong drink, he walked back outside and scooted the saucer into the corner. The cat finished the milk without taking its eyes off him, then disappeared across the roof.

"You're welcome," he said.

Thunder rumbled overhead, and it began to drizzle. Somewhere among the reports and weather charts was an envelope from Heather. If he was lucky enough to find it, it might just include her address.

He searched his apartment for the better part of an hour before he found the card. Inside, something about friendship was written in cursive. Beneath the card he discovered a scented rose-colored envelope complete with return address.

Determined to give the woman a generous piece of his mind, he grabbed the newspaper, pocketed the envelope and dashed through the rain toward his car. The afternoon had given way to evening, and the sky grew dark—a tempest in the making.

He slid behind the wheel and whacked the dash with his fist. A split instantly formed in the vinyl, and he swore at Heather under his breath. How dare she ruin his life in the pursuit of a salable story? She could have called before condemning him to a life of occupational purgatory. Damn her.

The wipers slapped back and forth. Halfway across town, he turned into a neighborhood of newer Mediterranean-styled townhouses. He found her place easily enough, a two-story stucco job flanked by palm trees.

He dried his face with his coat sleeve and caught a raindrop on his tongue. Perhaps he should have called. Screw it, she hadn't afforded him the same courtesy before releasing her incendiary weather story. He took a deep breath and proceeded toward the door.

Through an open window he could see the living room. Her furniture showed equal parts economy and good taste, the look one might fashion from one of those Scandinavian catalog stores. A push of the doorbell was followed a moment later by the sound of chimes and a woman's voice. "Just a minute."

The porch light came on and the door opened a crack, held in check by a short length of chain.

"What are you doing here?" she whispered.

Erik stood there, speechless. "We need to talk," he finally managed. "Inside."

The door closed. A moment later, the chain made a telltale rattle, and the door opened.

Heather stood there with her hair in a turban fashioned from a towel. She smelled like fresh apricots and gripped the top of her robe while urging him inside.

"I hope I didn't interrupt anything," he said, making his way through the door.

"What did you expect?"

Erik shrugged. "I've been calling for over a month and never heard back, and then I see this," he said, producing the newspaper headlining her story.

She fumbled with a cigarette and lighter.

"I didn't know you smoked."

She drew in a lungful of smoke and blew it in his direction. "Only when I'm nervous."

"And you're nervous now?"

"A little."

"Why didn't you return my calls?"

"Forget it, Erik. You should have left things the way they were."

"What about Augusta and that night at my place?"

"I think you'd better go," she said, glancing up the stairs and urging him back toward the door.

"Soon as you tell me why you went public with that story."

"The weather's fair game. If you don't have the guts to warn people about the danger, I do."

"There's a time and place."

"When? After the next storm slams ashore? Sorry, but I needed a breakout story, and I knew you'd never go along with it."

"So you slept with me to get information?"

"I have needs, same as you. Besides, you didn't seem to mind." She stood her ground like an alley cat with no intention of becoming somebody's pet.

Just then, hinges squeaked at the top of the stairs. Clutching the railing with one hand and a small blanket in the other, a young girl of three or four started down the steps.

"Mommy?"

Heather turned to Erik. "Now you've done it."

Whatever courage the vodka afforded him earlier had disappeared. He'd prepared himself for a battle, not this.

"Come on, honey," she said, "back to bed."

The little girl sucked on the corner of her blanket and did as she was told. She padded back up the stairs in her pajamas, staring over her shoulder as she went.

A moment later, Heather came back down the stairs. "Well, now you know. I'll do whatever it takes to keep a roof over my daughter's head. Besides, that story might just garner an award."

Erik couldn't shake the feeling he'd been betrayed. Still, he found himself wanting another chance with her. "I could have been fired."

"Look, I'm sorry you got hurt."

Heather's tough veneer began to give way, and Erik watched her shed a bona fide tear or two.

"You're a nice guy, Erik. You deserve someone better. I don't want to get in the way of that," she said, opening the door for him. "You see, the problem with us is me."

CHAPTER 22

The Golden State

The California coast was home to four National Weather Service field offices. By late Wednesday afternoon, Erik had finished up at the third site, the weather office in Oxnard.

After completing his meetings in Eureka, Monterey and Oxnard, he turned his attention to San Diego. He exited his motel room the following morning at a quarter of five and headed across the damp asphalt toward his rental car. The cool ocean air felt good against his face.

Two hours into the drive, the freeway merged with Highway 101 south and the Pacific. Overhead, the morning sky resembled the dark mottle of a turtle's back.

Somewhere in the vicinity of Camp Pendleton Marine Base he observed a cluster of telltale structures on the seaward side of the highway: a pair of large concrete domes and a smaller, lower profile one. A nuclear power plant from the looks of it, right at the ocean's doorstep.

The San Diego office of the National Weather Service wasn't actually located there. The office was located in a medium-sized suburb thirty minutes northeast, in the city of Rancho Bernardo. Housed in a lovely serpentine building constructed of terra cotta blocks curving along a hillside, the field office offered a stunning view of the mountains to the east and a pair of koi ponds below.

Erik let himself inside the lobby and moved down a hallway lined with weather photographs. Inside a command area, several middle-aged guys hunkered around computer screens. Beyond them, a window ran the entire length of the room.

One of the men swiveled around to face him, his hulk of a body all but burying the chair in which he sat.

"You Reynard?"

Erik nodded.

"We've been expecting you," the big man said, rising from his chair. "I'm Otto Winderman, Warning Coordination Meteorologist. Over there's Carl Hollinger. This here's Tim Bowne and next to him is Ben Martinez."

One by one, the crew turned from their computer screens. Hollinger stared wall-eyed at Erik and smiled, his good eye tracking his movement across the room. "Any relation to that hotshot specialist down at the Hurricane Center?"

"Guilty as charged."

"Nice work on those storm tracks," Hollinger said, looking on unfocusedly.

After the introductions, Erik followed Otto Winderman across the room. The meteorologist likely tipped the scales north of three hundred pounds. His rust-gray beard and forearm tattoos gave him the look of a hell-bound biker.

Although he looked like a bruiser, he spoke in the level tone of a quiet Midwesterner. It turned out he had migrated from Wisconsin's cheese country and drove a minivan.

"Can't beat the weather," he said, nodding toward the window. "You'd never get me back to the Midwest. I shoveled my last load of snow three years ago, Christmas Day. No sir, I'll stay right here, thank you very much. Come vacation time, the family piles into the van and we drive an hour and a half north. Got a little travel trailer in Huntington Beach."

Admitting that the California climate was indeed fine, Erik directed the conversation back to forecasting and advanced radars. "Where's the nearest NEXRAD site?"

"We call it the golf ball," Otto said, snatching a key ring from his desk. "It's located on a nearby hillside. I was just heading up there. Come along if you'd like."

Erik got an earful as Otto navigated the surrounding hills

and gave him a tour of the radar site.

"Information gets fed to us twenty-four hours a day, seven days a week, same as for your group down in Miami."

"What were those concrete domes I passed on the interstate? They looked like containment buildings."

"Good guess—the local utility built three reactors at that site."

"Operational?"

"Pull the safety rods and they'll crank out enough juice for a couple million homes."

"What about earthquakes?" Erik said. "And terrorists?"

"The facility's secure, at least the Nuclear Regulatory Commission claims it is. According to the power company, the plant's built to withstand a pretty good shaker, seven or so on the Richter Scale."

"You sound less than convinced."

"We did have a bit of a scare when a funnel cloud bore down on the plant. Those containment buildings are supposedly engineered to withstand wind speeds of a hundred-fifty miles per hour. A severe storm could, theoretically, exceed those limits."

"What about hurricanes?"

"Pretty rare out here, don't you think? Still, it got pretty tense back in '97 when Hurricane Linda came roaring up the coast. She was packing winds of one-ninety, strongest storm ever recorded in the eastern Pacific. If a storm like that ever makes landfall, those power plants will be the least of our worries. Damage from the flooding alone would be catastrophic."

Otto's warning underscored a genuine concern. After all, he was a scientist like himself, and he knew what he was talking about.

After finishing up at the NEXRAD site, they took lunch in town. Erik still had a couple of days to kill before heading to L.A. for his return flight home.

"So, what do you do around here when you're not watching the skies?"

"There's always Tijuana," Otto said, lowering his burger. "Some of the fellas like to head south for authentic Mexican food and cheap cervezas. Plenty of souvenirs, too, if you need something for the wife and kids."

With that, he flipped open his wallet to a family portrait of a heavyset woman, most likely Mrs. Winderman, and a couple of pie-faced kids.

"I can definitely see the resemblance. Your kids look just like you."

"How about you?"

Erik shook his head. "No wife, no kids."

"Sorry."

"Don't be."

"You could always head up to surf city, if you like your fun in the sun. You're welcome to use our beach trailer. Nothing fancy, but it's got hot water, TV and a fridge. It's just sitting out there collecting sand."

"I couldn't," Erik said, "but thanks."

"What about Catalina? There's an express cruiser leaves out of Long Beach."

Erik nodded at the possibility and tossed down some plastic. Perhaps Samuelson's fascination with island living had rubbed off on him—Catalina sounded intriguing. If he left Rancho Bernardo early, he might make the early morning crossing.

CHAPTER 23

Dedication day

The Department of Weather's landmark groundbreaking ceremony was scheduled for ten o'clock, eastern standard time, less than two miles from the White House. Washington can get pretty hot by late summer, and Robert Ocean was grateful the President had agreed to oblige him with an early appearance. According to the weather report, the day was shaping up to be a scorcher.

A battalion of uniformed police patrolled the street and set up barricades while K-9 units and Secret Service worked the perimeter of the cordoned-off site. Several suits wearing shades milled about sipping coffee, trying to act inconspicuous.

At the center of the site a platform had been erected, providing seating for fifty or so dignitaries. Near the front of the platform, a newly minted Department of Weather seal had been affixed to the front of a walnut podium. Nearby, a technician put the finishing touches on the public address system and tapped the microphone.

A mountain of freshly excavated soil behind the platform did little to keep out the sound of construction equipment working nearby.

Ocean glanced in Spicer's direction and nodded approvingly. His corporate counsel had apparently pulled all the right strings and generally done a rather magnificent job, guaranteeing the Department of Weather's design contract went to Dern,

Kilpatrick and Greene, exactly as instructed.

Bruner approached from behind a news van, clutching a gold-painted shovel. "Five minutes, Mr. Ocean."

"How do I look?"

"Distinguished," Bruner said, brushing a speck of lint from his boss's lapel.

Ocean turned to Spicer and whispered, "Perhaps you should mingle, do a little influence peddling."

"Very well," Spicer said, heading into the crowd like a finning shark.

Ocean stepped from the platform and beckoned Bruner to follow. Once beyond the news vans and outside camera range, his smile disappeared. "I've got a little job for you. There's an outspoken specialist down at the National Hurricane Center who may need a little persuading. His name's Reynard, cocky sonofabitch."

"Samuelson's friend?"

Ocean nodded. "He's been asking a lot of questions, claims his friend's trailer was ransacked by someone from the Department of Weather."

"What would you like me to do?"

"Have a look around his apartment. Dig up some dirt, see what you can find. There are gaps in Samuelson's research, those journals you found are incomplete. Perhaps Reynard knows something."

"Anything else?"

Ocean pulled a news clipping from his vest pocket and handed it to Bruner. "This feature story was written by a journalist down in Miami, an acquaintance of Reynard's, a real looker. Judging from this story she's angling for a Pulitzer. Offer her a television spot with our affiliate in Los Angeles. She won't be able to resist. And keep her on a short leash, we may need to censor her."

Bruner nodded.

"The less contact she has with Reynard, the better. We don't need the additional scrutiny."

By the time Ocean emerged from behind the news van, he was once again sporting his captivating smile. He waved to a group of onlookers gathered at the historic site and plunged the ceremonial shovel into a mound of dirt. Cameras flashed.

Several moments later, the presidential limousine squealed

around the corner, flags flapping atop the fenders. The limo angled toward the curb and came to a stop, flanked by several motorcycle cops and two Secret Service sedans.

Ocean squared his shoulders. It was almost time. He'd begun to think the President might stiff him, and that simply wouldn't do.

Spicer swapped an empty champagne glass for a fresh one and teetered toward his boss.

"Try not to get bombed," Ocean whispered through his teeth.

A Secret Service agent assigned to guard the limousine dashed toward the door, his shoulder holster clearly visible beneath his coat. He took hold of the door handle and pulled.

Ocean glanced at Bruner, who appeared to have a superior line of sight, and noticed a sudden change in his expression. The band struck up a familiar melody, hinting at the problem. For Ocean, a monumental problem. It wasn't Sanderson's "Hail to the Chief" as was customary with presidential visitations. Instead, the band played a military march.

This meant but one thing, and Ocean's heart began to sink. His fears were confirmed the moment the Vice President stepped from the limo. Refusing to allow his disappointment to show, he managed to remain smiling.

"Who does the President think he's messing with?" he snarled. "Some junior congressman from corn county? He wouldn't be sitting so high and mighty if it hadn't been for me."

"I don't understand," Bruner said. "We were told to expect the President."

"Well, he isn't here, is he?" Ocean said, eyes narrowing into slits.

"Unconscionable," Spicer said, spearing a morsel from a passing tray.

Despite his indignation, Ocean reluctantly put his hands together and joined the attendees in applause. If this was all his appointment meant, the President could just piss off. After all, he had his own fiefdom to govern. He was chairman of the nation's largest broadcasting company, for God's sake. He was also the Secretary of Weather and privy to sensitive data, classified satellite data.

CHAPTER 24

Spook

Gustav Bruner reached the Hurricane Center at midnight with enough contrived evidence to end a dozen careers. He snapped on a pair of smooth surgical gloves and went to work. Access to the Center proved easy—one of the exit doors had been deliberately left unlocked. Inside, the dimly lit corridor smelled of floor wax.

Bruner remained in the shadows as a floor polisher whirred in the distance. This wasn't the first assignment he'd taken on Ocean's behalf, and it wouldn't be the last. If anything went wrong, he could disappear instantly in a city the size of Miami and be back in Bloemfontein before anyone noticed he was gone.

A janitor hollered something in Spanish, and the sound of laughter echoed down the hall. A moment later, a second janitor mamboed across the floor to the beat of some red-hot salsa music, following the floor polisher's lead. Bruner flattened himself against a dark wall as a meteorologist working swing shift glanced up from his terminal.

Erik's office lay just ahead. Once inside, Bruner glanced around nervously and closed the door. He opened a bag he'd smuggled under his arm, poured a few ounces of vodka into a mug and stashed the half-empty bottle inside the desk drawer. A scout knife glistened in the open drawer, a ripe-looking orange atop the desk—he could smell it.

After opening the blade, he speared the orange and skillfully removed its skin in a long, continuous coil. The wedges were sweet, the entire fruit gone in less than a minute. He opened and closed the blade, then wiped it clean against his pant leg. The knife had a decent heft to it, the blade sharp and well cared for.

He slipped a compact disk into Erik's computer and uploaded counterfeit weather files, unauthorized Internet communiqués intended for the tabloids.

As the floor polisher came closer, Bruner removed the disk and inched down the hallway toward the director's office. After centering an envelope atop the desk, he ducked through the exit door and was gone.

CHAPTER 25

Catalina Island

Back in California, Erik strained to peer through the soup until the weather cleared near the intersection of Interstate 5 and Laguna Canyon Road.

Considering Hurricane Linda's near miss, Otto Winderman had every right to be concerned. A ridge of mountains encircled the Southern California basin like the lip of an enormous cauldron. If a monster storm made landfall, monsoon-like rains would produce widespread flooding, far too much runoff for the state's aging system of flood control channels to handle. But hurricanes in California? Even Samuelson dared not make such an assertion.

The killer storms he had predicted were more likely to occur along the Atlantic or in the Gulf of Mexico—perhaps New Orleans, which, according to some, was the most vulnerable target of all.

The visibility soon improved, and Erik watched an endless procession of cars materialize out of the fog, all the way into Los Angeles and beyond. Commuters lined up like devotees, beating their way toward Mecca. He observed the surrounding traffic and doubted most Californians could get anywhere very quickly, especially in the wake of a civil defense emergency.

He hated venturing too far from the Center at the height of the hurricane season. Still, the trip had done him good, helping him gain some long overdue perspective.

He thought about Samuelson during the long drive north, wondering how long he had struggled before the sea finally claimed him. Had he worn a lifejacket? Did he lose it? No body had been found, and that meant no dental records, no DNA.

The sea had its own methods of recycling. Perhaps some predator had rid the waves of him, before his lifeless body had bloated up with gas. Erik favored a different scenario, one of Samuelson simply letting go and slipping peacefully beneath the waves.

@

Later that morning, the Catalina-bound cruiser neared the mid-channel mark. Inside the roomy cabin, Erik inhaled the scent of salt air mixed with diesel exhaust. It reminded him of barnacles and back bays, of mussel-encrusted docks and low tide. The boat navigated the lumpy sea, lurching toward its destination.

Sea spray rained against the window, obscuring the view. Erik placed his hand against the warm glass and counted the droplets between his fingers.

Turning his attention back to the boat, he noticed a young woman with tightly braided hair smiling at him as she passed. He buried his head in a weather journal—guess he still had it, whatever it was.

Anxious for some news on the local scene, he circled the cabin collecting papers—local rags for the most part, dailies out of Long Beach, Avalon and San Pedro. Flopping back into his seat, he flipped to a section dedicated to the weather, where the forecast called for blue skies and balmy conditions.

What he read next was not so comforting: *SURFACE SEA TEMPS TOP AN UNPRECEDENTED 79 DEGREES FOR THIRD WEEK IN A ROW*. The report may have been good news for fishermen and sunbathers, but not for someone familiar with the dynamics of hurricanes. He decided to concern himself with the unseasonably warm seas upon his return to Miami and settled in for the duration of the trip.

The cruiser's seats were modern, like the ones used aboard jetliners. A party atmosphere prevailed on board, and a small group of tourists sporting straw hats and shell necklaces struggled to maintain their balance at a stand-up bar.

On the port side of the boat, a trophy wife in glitzy sunglasses clung to a rich old fart easily twice her age. Behind her were seated a group of Hawaiians, packing outrigger paddles.

Catalina was a favorite destination for southlanders: outrigger racing, kayaking, water-skiing and world-class diving.

A sailboat bobbed into view. A moment later, a shapely brunette moved to the helm and waved. Erik studied the boat, did a double take on the girl and thought maybe, just maybe, she was waving to him. He wished he were aboard, sailing off to some far-flung port.

For a fleeting moment he reminisced about Heather. He fantasized rubbing her shoulders with coconut oil and remembered where things had gone wrong. After all, he had about as much of a chance reconnecting with Heather as he did sailing off with the girl in the sailboat. The sailor girl's boyfriend climbed out on deck and their lips met, pretty much killing the fantasy.

Erik switched on a global positioning device and noted his location on a pocket map of the Pacific. Other islands linked together, up and down the predominantly blue page—San Miguel, Santa Rosa, Santa Cruz, Anacapa, San Nicholas and San Clemente. The map extended south into Mexico, past the Coronados to Guadalupe Island and beyond. But Catalina was the real pearl in the archipelago, an authentic island paradise a mere twenty-six miles from Los Angeles.

Catalina's jagged coastline loomed into view. Once the boat reached the protective lee of the island, the seas began to calm. Passengers gathered in the stern and prepared to disembark.

Erik perused the visitor's guide he had picked up prior to sailing. With its close proximity to Los Angeles, Avalon had once been a favorite playground for Hollywood's rich and famous— titans like Bogart, Stan Laurel and Oliver Hardy.

Perhaps the island's most prominent feature was its world-famous casino building—a huge, concrete, Moorish affair where the chewing gum folks who built the place used to invite a few hundred of their closest friends for a little dinner dancing to the sound of the big band greats. The casino was large enough to house the island's year-round population with ample provisions for a two-week stay.

The boat slowed to comply with the 5 MPH buoys encircling the harbor. Erik moved aft with his laptop computer over his shoulder and his roll-along bag in tow. After the docking lines were secure, he made his way up the gangway and down a cobblestone road bordering the bay.

With the harbor clear of sea mist, he could see from one end of Avalon to the other, the entire distance less than two miles. The town was awash with souvenir shops, restaurants and bars—festive cantinas crowded even before noon—places like the Blue Parrot, El Galleon, Descanso Beach and Antonio's. Joints like Shipwreck Joeys, Luau Larry's and the Chi Chi Club.

Erik slid past an open bar and followed a sign leading up the steps to his hotel. Ceiling fans turned overhead, giving the lobby a decidedly New Orleans flair. He flashed some plastic, stated his preference for an ocean view and was shown to his room by a fellow resembling a witness under one of the government's relocation and protection programs.

"How long you gonna be with us?"

"Just one night, I'm leaving tomorrow on the afternoon boat."

The clerk rolled a toothpick between his lips and pushed the door open with his pointy shoe.

"Here you go, home sweet home. Ice is in the lobby, behind the louvered door. You need anything else, give a holler."

Erik dispatched the man with a dollar.

"Gee," he said, snapping the bill between his fingers, "thanks a lot."

Anxious to sample one of the local cantinas, Erik slipped the room key into his pocket and made for the door. Halfway down the block, he found this quaint little hole-in-the-wall with an unobstructed view of the harbor. Above him, a black-and-white photograph showed Avalon in the grip of a major storm. Glancing across the tranquil harbor, he found it hard to believe it was the same place.

Slender palm trees in the picture's foreground bent nearly in half while huge waves exploded against a sea wall. He sat at a table beneath the photograph and flipped open the menu.

A waiter nodded in the direction of the picture. "Bet

you've never seen anything like that."

Erik simply smiled. After placing his order, he turned his attention back to the photograph. Judging from the agitated sea state, he figured the wind had been blowing sixty plus on the day the picture was taken, a decent storm at that.

Major storms may have been imminent, but where would they strike? Category 5 storms required vast oceans to feed upon—very large, very warm oceans. Covering an area of over a hundred-sixty-five million square kilometers, the Pacific was more than twice the size of the Atlantic and home to some of the deadliest storms of all, super typhoons.

There were notorious stretches of ocean out there, latitudes with ominous names like the Roaring Forties and Howling Fifties, vast oceanic graveyards boasting tremulous waves like the Screeching Sixties and Screaming Seventies.

Welcome to California. Mud slides and rain, maybe, but hurricanes? A cool breeze fanned his face, and he thought about Samuelson. At the very least he owed his old friend an unbiased assessment and vowed to have a careful look at his research upon his return to Miami.

The waiter arrived a moment later, balancing a platter on his arm: shrimp enchiladas oozing with tomatilla sauce, a stack of steaming tortillas and a frosty bottle of beer.

After a couple of cool ones, Erik felt pretty serene. He guessed the table in front of him stood a mere six or seven feet above sea level. It wouldn't take much of a storm surge to inundate downtown Avalon.

Erik tipped the waiter and hiked west on Via Casino, past the historic Tuna Club to a point where the road ended near the landmark casino building. It was a short walk back to midtown Avalon where he boarded a sightseeing bus driven by a man with an uncanny resemblance to Buffalo Bill Cody.

After visiting the island's impressive botanical gardens, the bus passed through town and climbed Stagecoach Road. Framed with eucalyptus trees and an occasional scruffy pine, the road afforded a grand panorama of the Pacific Ocean below.

They slowed for an unplanned photo stop as a dozen or so bison grazed below the road.

"Harry, look at the buffalo," said a woman in the front of the bus.

Never one to forget a voice, Erik looked up to see the same trophy wife in the big round sunglasses he'd observed earlier aboard the cruiser.

"A correction if I may," the driver said over the P.A. "The animals grazing to the left of the bus are popularly referred to as American bison. The scientific name, if you will, is Bison bison."

The tour was something of a yawn, but it beat hiking the nearly vertical trek up to Catalina's Airport-in-the-Sky.

Erik motioned toward a dusty intersection. "Where does that road lead?"

"Divide Road's a non-public road, property of the Catalina Conservancy. It doubles as a firebreak and runs all the way back to the botanical gardens. Over there's Mount Orizaba, the island's tallest peak at two-thousand-ninety-seven feet."

Before long, they slowed atop a sunny plateau. To the right was the terminal building and restaurant—beside it, the tower.

"Constructed in 1936, the airport opened for general aviation use in 1959. The blocks required for the terminal building's construction were produced by," the driver said with a bit of a lilt, "the Catalina Tile Company. It even withstood the big one, the '83 El Nino's freak ninety-five M.P.H. winds."

The air brakes hissed, the door opened and the tourists piled out for a potty break and cool refreshments inside the terminal. Erik used the opportunity to hike out to the edge of the plateau. Moderately steep cliffs punctuated each end of the runway, giving the impression the airport had been leveled from a mountain top.

@

It was early afternoon by the time Erik returned to downtown Avalon. On his hike back to the hotel, he watched small green waves lap the pilings beneath the pier—the same pier seriously threatened during the storm in the photograph.

He turned seaward and strode across the planks, past a dozen or so concessions toward a huge fish scale near the structure's end. A load block swung from the scale's wooden gallows.

A fishing boat idled beside a boarding area to offload its catch, its diesel engine burbling. Two back-slapping fishermen made their way toward the scale with a couple of burlap bags.

They emptied the bags onto the pier deck and out tumbled several large fish. They were substantially longer than the bags, with toothy maws and large predatory eyes.

"Where'd you catch those things?" asked an amazed onlooker. "Mexico?"

The fishermen began to laugh.

"Hell no," one of them said, pointing offshore. "We was out at the three-forty-two spot."

"Might as well broadcast it on the boob tube," said his friend. "Get your pictures, and let's get out of here."

A guy in a Hawaiian shirt snapped away with a digital camera while an officer from the Department of Fish and Game taped the length of the catch and asked to see licenses.

Erik watched the goings-on while enjoying a frozen banana he'd purchased at a nearby stand. He leaned against the pier rail and watched an old-timer work a shrimp jig through the water.

"Catch anything?"

"A couple of perch is all," said the man, motioning to a half-filled bucket, "picky little bastards."

The old-timer spit over the rail and glanced at the wahoo sprawled out on the planks. "Three-forty-two my ass."

"What's that?" said Erik.

"Those fish, they're wahoo. I don't think they've ever been taken in these waters. Maybe if you were down in Mexico, south of Roca Partida or trolling past some tropical atoll. But not here, not Catalina Island."

A swarm of flies soon discovered the catch, and the fishermen worked the wahoo back into the bags.

For Erik, the discovery proved intriguing. He caught up with the fishermen as they boarded the boat. "Mind if I ask you a question?"

The more outspoken of the two ignored him completely

and hoisted the bags aboard. The other fisherman turned to face him. "What do you want to know?"

"Shuddup, Frank, ain't you said enough already?"

Erik stepped onto the boat's swim step and leaned across the transom, feeling the rumble of the engine beneath his feet.

The agitated fisherman lifted a gaff from its holder and spun toward him. "Are you still here?"

"Relax," Erik said, flashing his credentials. "I'm with the Department of Weather. I just want to ask a few questions."

The fisherman eased the gaff back into its holder and stepped close enough to read his ID. "Mister, you've got thirty seconds."

"Did you really take those fish in local waters?"

"If it's all the same to you, I don't want every pinhead with a rod and reel out here."

"Guaranteed confidential."

The fisherman stalled for a moment and looked around. "We must've been down seventy feet or more. We'd just baited-up a couple live mackerel when they hit. Those big bastards really smoked our reels."

The prospect of a vast body of warm water seventy feet deep was sobering indeed. Upon his return to Miami, he'd check with Tai, to confirm the sea temps being reported.

He thanked the fishermen for their time and hiked back down the pier toward his hotel.

By the time Sunday afternoon rolled around, Erik found himself back aboard the Catalina cruiser, snapping pictures. He'd picked up some additional baggage along the way: a tee shirt boasting a smiling shark and an eight-by-ten glossy of Avalon Harbor at the height of the storm.

Changes in surface sea temperatures meant profound changes in ocean upwellings thousands of miles away. Currents capable of bringing forth exotic fish might bring forth other things as well—exotic things like hurricanes.

CHAPTER 26

Barbarians at the door

Erik's troubles began the moment he sailed through the Hurricane Center's doors. A guard resembling an oil drum lowered a half-eaten doughnut and maneuvered in front of him with a smudge of powdered sugar still on his chin. Of particular interest was the Ocean Broadcasting logo stitched to the pocket of his uniform.

"Sorry, you're not allowed in here."

"I work here," Erik said, spotting the revolver at his side. "When did you guys start packing?"

"Ever since security was breached. You have any other questions, you'll have to ask the director."

Erik had the urge to sneak past the guard until he spotted the nightstick.

"No problem, you're the one with the billy club and popgun. Tell you what, I'll wait here while you find Deevers. Tell him his top specialist wants to have a word with him."

The guard drew his nightstick and tapped it against his palm. "I know who you are, Doctor Reynard. Any trouble, and I was told to show you the door."

"That's enough," Deevers said, moving briskly down the hall.

For the first time in his life, Erik was actually happy to see him. Perhaps he could explain a few things, like what was meant by *security breach*.

"If you weren't so damn talented, I wouldn't care, but to throw away your career like it was nothing. Why?"

Erik looked on, quizzically. What the hell was he talking about?

"I warned you about leaking this severe weather stuff," Deevers said, producing a computer disk. "And the drinking, Erik. For God's sake get some help."

"What are you trying to say?"

"What he means is you've got ten minutes to clear out your office," said the guard.

Erik refused to dignify the comment, looking instead to Deevers.

"I'm sorry," he said, turning back up the hall. "It's out of my hands."

@

The guard stood watch outside Erik's office while he packed his things, seven archive boxes in all. One item was missing, the Boy Scout knife he kept in his desk drawer. He was tearing through his desk drawers searching for the pocketknife when Tai suddenly appeared in the open doorway.

"I'm glad you're here," he said, urging her inside. "Somebody's got it in for me, they set me up."

She looked at him sympathetically. "Promise me you'll get some help."

"Help with what?"

"With the drinking, Erik. Isn't that what got you fired?"

He held her by the shoulders and stared into her eyes. "What about Samuelson, was that because of my drinking? How about the lack of an advanced warning the night before he went missing?"

She studied him with sad, sorrowful eyes.

"You're probably suspect, too," he warned. "We worked together, surely they know that. I need some time to sort things out. I'm heading back to California."

"Rooming with Heather?"

"What are you talking about?"

"I thought you knew, she took a job with Ocean Broadcasting in Los Angeles."

Erik stood there, dumbfounded. He fished his wallet out of his jeans and handed Tai a business card. "I need all the data you can gather from our buoy network. Send it to Otto Winderman. His number's on the card, he'll know how to reach me."

CHAPTER 27

Fossils in the freezer

There wasn't much keeping Erik in Miami, not anymore. He longed to be back at the Hurricane Center where his fascination with storms had been inspired. He missed Samuelson, and he was beginning to feel more than a little sorry for himself.

After setting the parking brake outside his apartment, he stepped from the Saab clutching a brown paper bag and slammed the door shut with his hip.

The sound of the car door carried to Erik's apartment where Gustav Bruner froze in the shadows. He shot across the living room and peered through the drapes. Trouble was on the way. He'd have to leave, taking only what he could carry.

Bruner rummaged through a roll top desk, searching for Samuelson's notes, when a big orange cat leapt onto the kitchen counter and knocked a beer bottle into the sink. He spun around, clutching the pocketknife. The blade glistened, sharp and fit for skinning. The cat hissed, staring at him with molten amber eyes.

Glancing toward his apartment, Erik gave the paper bag a hoist and started up the stair. The vodka bottles clinked, three liters in all—more than enough to transport him to a place where nothing much mattered. Glancing at the soft yellow light streaming through an open window, he climbed the last few steps where parrots and palm trees had been rendered in a mosaic of splintered tile. He gripped the wrought iron handrail and considered his rocky career. One thing was certain: his presence at the Hurricane Center had certainly made someone pretty damned uneasy.

Good old by-the-book Deevers, ever the obedient pencil pusher. It wasn't really his fault. Once he'd been tipped off about the vodka and the falsified press leaks, what else could he have done? Erik slid his key into the lock. Whoever was responsible for setting him up had correctly anticipated the director's response.

Erik's feelings toward Heather were quite another matter. She now had the one thing she'd always wanted: a high profile job in broadcasting. He'd been the unwitting agent for her advancement, and he felt used. A half turn to the right and click, the door unlocked.

@

Bruner heard the workings of the lock and realized it was too late to exit through the living room window. Deciding to take care of Dat Kat later, he closed the pocketknife. Using his fingertips for eyes, he moved down the dark hallway. He tried the bathroom window, only to find it painted shut.

As the front door opened, he slid unseen into the bedroom. Desperate for a place to hide, he eased open the closet door and squeezed inside. It would have to do. Finding space behind a wall of clothes, he tried his best to make himself small and rolled the knife around in his palm. He would wait there all night if he had to.

@

Erik locked the door behind him and moved toward the kitchen. He lowered the bag into the sink and stared at the open window. Strange, he didn't remember leaving it open. Suddenly, the alley cat shot out of the darkness.

"Where in the hell did you come from?" he said, moving toward the window to close it. "You must be hungry."

The refrigerator yielded an unopened bottle of vodka mix and a half can of tuna. He spooned the remaining fish into a small bowl and set it on the floor, then lifted the vodka out of the bag. After closing the blinds, he placed two bottles in the cupboard before breaking the seal on a third.

Standing in front of the fridge, he dropped a handful of ice into a mug bearing the insignia of his alma mater. He filled it two-thirds with vodka, topped it off with a splash of Bloody Mary mix and leaned against the sink.

A third of the mug disappeared with the first hoist. Wanting to remain undisturbed, he gripped the phone cord and yanked, soundly disconnecting it at the wall. He left the limp cord where it fell and topped off his mug.

One of these days the Hurricane Center would need his help. He imagined a panicky call from Deevers at the height of a serious storm, the next Andrew or Camille.

Forecasting wasn't just about advanced radar systems and computer modeling. It had a human side, and the best forecasting required instinct, intuition and a little bit of luck.

He whipped off his jacket and pitched it into a lumpy leather chair. Who was he kidding? His career had been blown apart like a smoke ring in a typhoon.

A telltale creak emanated from the end of the hall, and he felt his body stiffen. Turning an ear in the direction of the sound, he listened. It was the kind of sound that makes the spit dry up in your mouth and turns your knees to rubber.

A moment later, the familiar bang of water hammer was followed by the groan of old plumbing inside the wall. Probably nothing, he thought, most likely his neighbor, Mrs. Zambrano, running her evening bath.

No sooner had he stepped inside the living room than he noticed something disturbing. The front of his roll top desk was up, and his papers were scattered. Someone had been inside his apartment, and, judging from his desk, they'd left in a hell of a hurry.

Erik took a quick inventory. Everything was accounted for, save for some non-critical precipitation tables he'd been compiling.

He moved toward an overflowing bookshelf where he'd crammed Samuelson's package beneath the local yellow page directory. He had no idea who had ransacked his friend's trailer. They were obviously looking for something, probably his journals or the prehistoric pollen and fossilized coral samples inside the package.

Back in the kitchen, he stashed the package in the most unlikely place he could think of, the freezer. He crept toward the front closet where he kept a white ash, Louisville Slugger—a memento from his father. Weighing the bat in his hands, he strolled down the hall.

He flipped on the bathroom light and had a look inside the shower. Nothing. Next, he moved to the spare bedroom. After giving the room a careful once-over, he stood in front of the closet and eased open the door. He rammed the blunt end of the bat into a wall of hanging clothes, then crossed the hall to his own room. Down on all fours, he peered beneath the bed: some old socks, a few dusty books and a year's worth of Weatherwise Magazine.

The agitated alley cat mewed at his side. Erik stared at the closet doors and felt his heart beating fast. Slowly, he reached out to take hold of a pair of seahorse-shaped knobs and pulled.

No room for anyone in there, he thought, whipping through the hangers. When he got to the coats, he raised the bat and jabbed it headlong into a mass of parkas and leather. The coast was clear. There was just one thing left to take care of.

@

Above the closet, a small hatch remained hidden beneath fifty years of paint and a torn curtain of cobwebs. The only way up was to climb a shoe tree conveniently fastened to the back wall of the closet.

The cramped space was hot and filled with dusty air. Bruner crouched above the hatch, contorted as a yogi and still as a gargoyle. He glanced down at his luminous watch dial and smiled. He'd make his move soon enough.

@

Erik downed the rest of his drink. He grabbed his bat and stormed back inside the spare bedroom where the modeled cityscape lay before him, his pride and joy. His head began to swim, and he reared back to take his best shot. "Screw it!"

Balsa wood exploded on impact, and buildings were sent splintering into the walls. The precisely scaled cityscape which had taken him months to build was gone in a matter of seconds. Satisfied with the level of destruction, he killed the lights on his way through the doorway. Deevers was right—Samuelson's theories had gotten him nowhere but fired.

Back in the kitchen, he poured more vodka and squeezed the half-empty bottle into the freezer. The room began to spin, and he shuffled off to bed. He didn't bother changing into his pajamas, simply closed his eyes and prayed the spinning would stop.

CHAPTER 28

Green tea at dawn

Erik awoke to the whistle of a tea kettle and a face full of fur. The big orange cat sat at his side, lording over the room like the Sphinx over Giza. The sound of footsteps swished across the carpet, only he was too hung over to do much about it. The mere thought of getting to his feet caused his head to pound.

The overhead light came on like the sun, catching him square in the retina.

"Go away," he groaned, dispatching the cat with a sweep of his arm and drawing the pillow down tight.

Besides the whistling tea pot came the sound of humming. A strange odor permeated the room, the scent of stewed kelp.

"Who's there?" he demanded.

With the pillow over his head, all he could see was a pair of legs from the waist down—charcoal slacks, dark socks and the same infernal humming.

"Erik-san?" came the familiar voice. "Are you awake?"

His face rose slowly from beneath the pillow. Yoshida... Christ, what was he doing there? The shower began with a whoosh, and a moment later the professor emerged from the bathroom, clapping his hands.

"Come," he said, "a shower will do you good. After that, I'll give you a cup of my special green tea. Chop-chop."

Erik sniffed the air. "Think I'm gonna puke."

"Is very best tea," said Yoshida, "Gyokuro tea. My sister

ships it to me from Shizuoka. It grows in the mountains, near the headwaters of the Oi River. You try, you see."

Erik mumbled something indecipherable and shuffled toward the bathroom. Beneath the oscillating spray of the shower, his head began to clear, and with clarity came the pounding of a world-class hangover.

He reached the kitchen a few minutes later dressed in a robe. "How'd you get in here, anyway?"

"The door was unlocked."

"That's impossible. I distinctly remember locking it," Erik said, then sneezed. "I walked in, locked the door and carried a grocery bag into the kitchen."

"Are you sick?"

"No, it's this damn cat. I think I'm allergic. Say, are you looking for a cat? You can have him if you want."

Yoshida declined.

"Samuelson's research!" Erik yelled, spinning toward the fridge. "Don't ask, it seemed like the last place a vandal would look."

He yanked open the refrigerator door and had a look around: a wedge of cheese, a half-dozen brown eggs, some bottled hot peppers and a carton of milk that had turned to yogurt. Next, he whipped open the freezer door.

"I'm afraid you're not making much sense," Yoshida said, curiously. "What would someone want with weather research?"

"That's a very good question," Erik said, dislodging an ice cube tray to free the package. "I asked myself the same thing when I realized someone had gone through my desk."

Strange, he could have sworn he'd left the open bottle of Stoly in there, too. He couldn't have been that far gone, or could he? The pounding in his head grew more intense, and he turned toward the cupboard for a little hair of the dog that bit him. One small problem—those bottles had vanished, too.

"Tea?" Yoshida said.

Staring into the sink, Erik spotted three empty vodka bottles jammed neck down in the drain.

"What in the hell did you do?" Erik said, pushing past him. "What gives you the right to come in here and play nursemaid? I don't remember asking for your help."

Yoshida ignored him. He appeared considerably more interested in Samuelson's research.

"Did you hear me?"

"Somebody needs to look after you. Talent is a terrible thing to waste. Besides, I promised Samuelson..."

The elder scientist stopped before detailing the promise he had made, and Erik felt the hostility flow out of him like air from a rapidly deflating balloon.

"I need your help," Yoshida said, "and I need you sober. Both Samuelson and I had predicted the coming changes. His notes may offer a clue." Yoshida glanced up solemnly. "I'm afraid the weather's likely to get much worse before it gets better."

Erik lifted the cup to his lips and sipped. The tea was as sobering as Yoshida's warning.

"The Eastern Pacific's the area I'd be worried about," he said, rummaging through the icy package. "Catch."

Yoshida plucked the sample out of the air. "What is it?"

"It's coral, a prehistoric carbonate—an archive into the past. I think that sample holds a clue."

"Has it been carbon dated?"

"Wouldn't do you much good. Carbon dating is good for 30,000 years, tops. I sent that sample to a forensic geologist for analysis. She claims it's a ringer for some deep-sea corals dating back over 400 million years. There's something here all right, something Samuelson wanted us to find, clues to a catastrophic weather shift. Towards the end, that's all he would talk about."

Yoshida held up the coral and closely examined it.

"Samuelson collected that sample near New Guinea, half a world away from the deep-sea deposits."

"How'd they get there?"

Erik shrugged. "That's a question I would have liked to have asked him."

Over the next few days, Yoshida shared details of his own findings. Erik sorted through Samuelson's notes and chipped away at fossilized coral samples, more convinced than ever of impending calamity. Still, the big question remained: where and when would monster storms strike? The spike in California sea temps was one clue worth pursuing.

Erik slid out the front door with a duffel bag slung over his shoulder and his suitcase in hand. Outside in the street, his trusty Saab waited: new fan belt, oil change, two new Pirellis, a six-dollar car wash and several strips of electrical tape over the telltale crack in the dash.

He'd prepaid the rent, stopped the paper and was preparing to lock the door when he witnessed an unbelievable sight: his elderly neighbor, Mrs. Zambrano, sitting outside in the morning sun with the big orange cat purring in her lap like a kitten.

The feline looked at him contentedly, eyes half-closed.

"I can't believe he lets you pet him. It took me weeks to get that close."

"I have a secret," she whispered, lifting a small package wrapped in butcher paper. "Smoked fish, he couldn't resist. A little kindness goes a long way."

Erik smiled—it did, indeed.

"Come here, meatball," he said.

Mrs. Zambrano stared at the suitcase in his hand. "Are you moving?"

"I'll be gone a while."

"What about the cat?"

"Right," he said, "the cat. Say, you wouldn't know the way to the Humane Society, would you?"

"Humane Society?" she said, her eyes welling up with concern. "I'd be happy to look after him. He'll be no bother, no bother at all."

Erik gratefully agreed to leave the cat in the old woman's care and folded a crisp new twenty into her palm. "For cat food."

CHAPTER 29

Storm watch

The first appreciable rain to hit the nation's heartland came in the form of a severe thunderstorm blackening the sky over much of Texas. Erik had just passed through Weatherford, traveling west on Route 66, when the rain began to fall. Huge cumulonimbus clouds gathered along the horizon like dusty freight cars.

He flipped on a hand-held weather radio and tuned in a local broadcast. A low-pressure center had pushed in from the northwest, colliding with dry southerly air and warm humid air from the Gulf. One glance out the window confirmed it was a recipe for heavy weather. From the looks of things, the nation's midsection was about to get a reprieve from the long-standing drought.

Later that afternoon at his motel, Erik tuned in the news. The broadcast was interrupted by a national weather bulletin. He sat on the edge of the bed and watched with the rapt attention of a kid at a matinee. All was not well. A hurricane had been born, the strongest of the season. Her name was Gert, and she'd already been classified as a Category 4. At eight hundred miles across, the storm was enormous. He felt certain she'd make the big leagues, and the hurricane became an immediate obsession.

He buzzed the Weather Service office in Rancho Bernardo and asked to be patched through to Otto Winderman.

"I've been expecting your call," Otto said. "I've got a package down here with your name on it. It's from the Hurricane

Center."

"Can you hold it for me?"

"Where are you?"

"I'm heading west on Route 66 and hitting some heavy weather."

"Calm as can be out west."

"Not for long," Erik said. "By the way, I need a place to stay. Is your trailer still available?"

Otto obliged, giving him directions to the trailer and the location of the hidden key.

"Before you stick your neck out, there's something you should know," Erik said. "Deevers gave me my walking papers."

"What the hell happened?"

"I'll tell you all about it when I get there. In the meantime, let's keep this termination business between us."

"You got it, friend."

During the last leg of his trip Erik turned south on Pacific Coast Highway. Otto's directions were right on the mark, and he slowed near the Huntington Beach Pier to gaze out at the Pacific.

Farther south he spotted a sign: Driftwood Shores Mobile Home Park. He took a hard left and idled between a pair of double-wides. There didn't appear to be anything mobile about the place—manufactured homes rested on pylons, and trailers squatted on flattened tires. This was apparently the end of the line.

He kept an eye out for Otto's trailer and pulled into a space with the Winderman coat-of-arms emblazoned on a metal mailbox. Once inside the powder blue coach, he flipped open his laptop and patched through to the Tropical Prediction Center's website.

Gert was pushing the upper limits of Category 4 territory with winds topping one-fifty. Erik did some preliminary calculations and wondered if he'd made a mistake leaving Miami.

The following morning, Erik rose early for his run. A recent spike in inland valley temperatures and corresponding intensification of the Catalina Eddy resulted in an unusually strong onshore flow—in other words, it was foggy.

He reached the end of the shrouded pier, unwound a length of string and lowered a weighted thermometer over the side. Later, back at the trailer, he noted the simmering sea temp in his journal. Still rising.

One of Winderman's kids had left behind a stack of surfing magazines which Erik eagerly consumed, catching up on the latest idiomatic beach speak. It was enough to make him want to throw down some major coin, score a gun and do some heavy rhino chasing. He'd tried surfing a couple of times before, but it took him a week to pull the residual board wax out of his chest hair. The yearning for an adrenal rush soon passed, and he ended up catching a latte near the pier and watching the morning sun burn slowly through the mist.

When he returned to the trailer, he discovered an urgent E-mail from Tai—something about a premonition. Despite a southeasterly shift away from the coast, Gert was keeping the Hurricane Center at its highest stage of alert.

CHAPTER 30

High noon

The Lockheed WC-130 shimmied as it closed in on the storm. Michael peered out the cockpit window and studied the ocean below. Based on all available data, the hurricane was expected to reach Category 5 status, what forecasters back in Miami affectionately referred to as catastrophic.

From an altitude of two miles, phenomenal sea waves appeared no more dangerous than streaks of foam across a turtle's back. But Michael knew better, realizing they stood an infinitely better chance up in the clouds than at sea level.

Their flight plan had taken them cautiously out and around Cuban airspace. A barometric low opened up over the Caribbean with the pressure falling fast.

First-hand storm observations flooded in from a wide area. The Coast Guard reported that a fishing boat overtaken earlier by the storm had lost their rudder in huge seas. When a rescue helicopter reached the site of their last transmission, all they found were some floating trash bags, a life ring and an active, category 1, Precision 406 EPIRB, its strobe light flashing in the waves.

Specialists at the National Hurricane Center correctly labeled the storm when its northerly track first carried it out of the tropics. When the storm blinked its telltale eye and cranked its wind speed up to 74 MPH, they knew exactly what it was—a hurricane, and a big one at that.

No sooner had Gert officially been classified as a hurricane than she turned and ducked beneath the Tropic of Cancer. The Florida coastline was off the list of potential targets, at least for now.

Michael checked his watch, confirming they were right on schedule. Beyond the Leeward Island of Antigua, he banked slightly, adjusting his course. Bands of feeder clouds spiraled towards the atmospheric whirlpool from hundreds of miles away.

Inside the cockpit, the crew studied non-stop satellite downloads spooling in from NESDIS. One unmistakable feature served to remind them of what they were dealing with, the hurricane's well-defined eye.

"Hell of a storm," said Martini.

Michael shot back a confident grin. "Twenty bucks says we'll be home in time for tonight's game."

"You're on," Martini said, "and I hope to hell you're right."

The copilot appeared to appreciate Michael's optimism. The last transmission out of Keesler included an uncustomary warning, "Be careful up there, boys."

Michael kissed Tai's photo for luck and clipped it to his flight plan.

@

Time: fifteen-hundred. Michael studied the cockpit gauges. The plane had taken a real rivet-loosening on its trip through the eyewall, the roughest ever.

They sailed around inside the eye, until the Aerial Reconnaissance Weather Officer's voice came over the mike.

"We're looking pretty good right here," he said, "release the dropsonde."

The slender missile sailed toward the sea, and the Hercules banked inside the eye. The worst part of flying into hurricanes was fighting your way back out of them. Catastrophic hurricanes were pretty damn rare, and that was fine with Michael. It had been a rough trip, and the return flight home would be no easier.

Quietly reminding himself of the enormity of his responsibility, he glanced around the cabin. The crew under his command had families. They had mortgages and backyard barbecues, and it was his job to get the plane back in one piece.

Gert's unsurpassed fury made it nearly impossible to stay on course, and the navigator almost missed the eye altogether.

Michael kept the wing tip just inside the wall of blackness, circling them at fun house speed. The Hercules felt flimsy as a plastic plane dropped in a washing machine stuck on spin. The wall of high velocity wind bordering the eye was dark and well-defined, appearing more solid than gaseous. Michael pinched the bridge of his nose and squinted to see through the windshield, preparing to make a go of it.

Over the radio came a warning, news that a second plane sent in to relieve them had been ordered back to base. Wind speeds in the eyewall had intensified. Unfortunately, Michael and his crew didn't have the luxury of waiting out the storm—their fuel was limited.

The crew instinctively tightened their safety harnesses. Sustained winds had been clocked at better than one-ninety, well into Cat 5 territory. Making matters worse was the fact that the storm was still spinning up.

Suddenly, everything went black and the Hercules shuddered. Tightening his grip on the controls, Michael fought to maintain his heading. He drew a breath and felt a sudden rumble, the doors to Hades opening wide. The shaking intensified, and he thought he saw rivets popping free.

"How long you think we're gonna be in this slop?" Martini asked.

"Hell if I know," Michael said. "Tell you what, this sonofabitch is big."

Water buried the windshield, and a loud pop resonated through the cockpit.

"What was that?" Martini yelled, staring wide-eyed at the gauges.

"Not sure," Michael said, straining at the yoke. "Check it out."

Lights flashed as all hell proceeded to break loose.

"I'm getting a lot of vibration here," Martini shouted.

Michael watched the plummeting tachometer as engine

four's fire handle lit-up.

"Shit!" Martini swore, eyes roving across the glare shield. "We've got total turbine and compressor failure, I'm shutting down number four."

He pulled the fire handle. No sooner had the fire switch killed the fuel to the troubled engine than an explosion burst the cowling. The engine began shucking its guts, and turbine blades flew like shrapnel.

Michael saw flames where engine four used to be until a burst of Halon flooded the fire.

Martini checked the gauges and stared outside at the punctured wing. "We're losing a lot of fuel."

Tightening his grip on the yoke, Michael struggled for control. He felt a strange imbalance as the Hercules began to yaw. Another fire handle light up.

"Kill three," he said, "looks like it's blown out, too."

Wind throttled the disabled aircraft, and Martini did as he was told. A moment later, the propeller feathered and went flat pitch as the engine shut down.

Michael applied more rudder to prevent all-out yaw. As the starboard tank neared empty, the weight imbalance between the wings became more pronounced. The left side of the aircraft now supplied a hundred percent of the fuel and power, and he had to struggle with the controls to keep the plane aloft.

Getting safely out of the hurricane with all systems operational was tough enough; flying crippled was suicide. Out of the corner of his eye, Michael observed his co-pilot crossing himself. He couldn't blame him. If there was ever a time to invoke divine intervention, this was it.

More turbine blades were thrown. Supersonic engine parts made a terrible shearing sound as they ripped through the plane. The altimeter spun like a roulette wheel, and tachometers died. They were losing altitude faster than fuel now.

Martini got on the radio, his voice edged with panic. He identified the plane, gave their coordinates and repeated the message again and again. "Come in Keesler, over."

Michael watched a perfectly good man hit his breaking point.

"Jesus," said Martini, "isn't anyone out there?"

Maintaining his cool, Michael said, "Get those escape hatches open, in case the fuselage buckles on our way in."

"Right," Martini said, unbuckling his harness and scrambling to his feet. He lowered the forward hatch and called aft, "Get those hatch covers down and stash them. Now!"

Michael secured Tai's photo inside his vest pocket and struggled to keep the plane aloft. Images of Tai, his mother and auntie bounced around inside his head. He could almost hear Tai's voice, cursing him if he didn't make it.

"Damn this storm," he whispered, pushing the plane into a dive. "Damn it!"

He glanced out the window. Thank God they still had wings— damn ragged, but they were wings. If the plane stalled, it would all be over in seconds. Rescuers would have to comb the sea floor with tweezers. He had to keep the plane in the air, keep it flying at all costs.

Through the windshield, it looked like they were going straight in.

Martini was back on the mike. "Mayday, Mayday!"

"Brace yourselves," Michael hollered, dropping the nose a few more degrees.

Waves zoomed into view. They were the size of small office buildings and breaking. If he timed it just right, he'd pull the nose up, belly onto a cresting wave and pray the drag would slow the plane before it slammed into the next oncoming swell. It wasn't much, but it was all they had.

"Get ready to shut down engines one and two," he yelled. "Kill them on the count of one."

Martini's hands hovered near the controls as the plane roared toward the sea. Michael began his short countdown. A moment later, Martini killed the remaining engines.

Michael pulled back on the yoke. The plane shook as the nose began to rise. Beneath them, the waves seemed to draw their enormity right out of the surrounding sea.

"Hold on!" Michael yelled. "We're going in!"

The Hercules bellied into the first wave with explosive force and remained airborne. It glided another quarter mile before slamming into a second wall of water. The right wing tore free on impact, and the Hercules careened sideways toward an even larger wave, an oncoming fifty-footer.

Michael buried his face in the crook of his arm as terrified moans filled the aircraft. The plane twisted out of control, and a wrenching sound preceded the separation of the tail section. The Hercules slammed into the wall of water and instantly foundered. Lights twinkled beneath the surface as the plane sank quickly out of sight.

CHAPTER 31

Missing in action

Erik returned from his morning run and switched on the television, an early seventies model with a lighted channel dial and UHF. After noting the rising sea temperature in his journal as he had the previous day, he headed for the fridge and rooted around for something to drink. He rose a moment later with a bottle of one of those fancy fruit teas.

The vintage TV struggled to conjure up an image, so he wrestled with the rabbit ear antennae to help it along. Slowly, the picture came into focus. An attractive blonde sat at a news desk straightening papers while the words Special Report marched across the bottom of the screen in large italics.

Erik fell backwards in his chair. Heather's voice was like a fingerprint, as unmistakable as DNA. She'd apparently gotten her big break the moment his life entered demolition mode. Just when he thought his jaw couldn't possibly fall any farther, she delivered news that sent it down another notch.

One of the planes from the 53rd Weather Recon Wing was reportedly missing in the vicinity of the storm. During the night, Gert pummeled the Leeward Islands of Barbuda and Antigua before turning south. Names of the missing crew members had been withheld until the families could be notified, and the Coast Guard promised an exhaustive search.

Later that morning, the telephone rang. It was Tai.

"Erik?"

"How did you find me?"

She was silent a long time.

"Otto Winderman," she managed at last, her voice shaky. "You gave me his card, remember? You said he'd know where to find you. Have you seen the news?"

"Not Michael," he said. "Oh, God, tell me it wasn't his plane."

She began to cry. "He had an interview scheduled next week with Delta, down in Atlanta. We spent all day, Saturday, looking at houses."

"I'm sorry."

"He gave me a ring, Erik, it's lovely."

"I'm sure it is."

"They say we should remain hopeful, that we should pray, that sometimes these things work themselves out. But those seas, Erik, I mean, how could they...?"

"Michael's a great pilot. If anyone could bring that plane in safely, he could."

"I've got some vacation time coming. I'm leaving tonight for Biloxi, to be with his family."

"Call me if you hear anything," he said in a reassuring voice, "anything at all."

Erik lowered the phone and hiked back toward the beach. He trudged through the sand, gazing west, unable to accept the fact Michael was gone. All this business about hope and prayer and beating the odds, who were they kidding? The storm had already reached Category 5 status by the time Michael had flown into it.

⑥

The drive to the Weather Service office in Rancho Bernardo took about ninety minutes. Once inside, Erik shot up the stairs two at a time. The sound of overworked computer printers filled the office.

Winderman surprised him from behind. "Take your coffee black?"

"Thanks."

"I guess you heard about that missing plane?"

Erik nodded. "The pilot was a friend of mine."

Otto shook his substantial head back and forth. "I spoke to one of your associates, a forecaster named Tai Jeffers. I gave her your number, hope that's okay?"

"She's the missing pilot's fiancée."

"Poor kid," Winderman said, tossing Erik a mailing bag held together with strapping tape. "She sent you this."

Erik slit open the package and found a month's worth of data from NOAA's web of offshore buoys.

"Looks like you've got your work cut out for you."

Suddenly, a meteorologist came wheeling around the corner. "Get this, the Hurricane Center just reported losing the storm, said it just disappeared. Can you beat that? No satellite recon, no NEXRAD, nothing—like the damn thing never existed."

"They lost it?" Erik said. "What do they mean it just disappeared? That's impossible. How in the hell do you lose a half-million-square-mile storm? Tell them to contact NESDIS and run a check on GOES 8."

"Right," said the meteorologist, "like they're gonna listen to me."

"You don't lose a hurricane like the keys to the family wagon. Who in the hell's in charge down there?"

"You know perfectly well who's in charge," Otto said. "He's the reason you're here, remember?"

"Thanks for reminding me."

Erik dropped into a chair and brought his fist up to his chin. Redundant systems didn't just fail—not simultaneously, and not without a little help. Lately, there had been far too many coincidences and even fewer explanations. He couldn't help but wonder how the lack of storm reconnaissance would hamper the Coast Guard's ongoing search-and-rescue efforts.

"Do you have room for me around this place?"

"You can use Tim Bowne's desk," Winderman said. "He's out all week. You need anything, just ask."

Two days passed before the hurricane was picked up again by weather satellite. No sooner had the storm done the improbable than the casualty and damage assessments began to roll in. Gert had ripped her way through Colombia before emerging in the Pacific. There was no shortage of fuel in the tepid seas, and the hurricane gorged itself on moist air over the tropics.

Word out of Colombia was catastrophic: thousands feared dead as mud slides buried dozens of villages and rain-induced flooding decimated the nation's coffee crop—by all accounts a level of devastation that would be felt for decades.

The moment the hurricane entered the Pacific, the National Hurricane Center retired the name Gert, like the jersey number of some venerable athlete. It became the third hurricane in a hundred years to occupy both oceans, and the most destructive ever recorded in the eastern Pacific. The press began referring to the hurricane simply as X. They didn't know what else to call it.

CHAPTER 32

Blast from the past

The hurricane continued to spin farther north, into the blue waters off the southern coast of Mexico. What it lost in overall size, it more than made up for in intensity. Mexico had thus far been spared the dragon's bite, but not the whip of its tail, the unrelenting rains.

The monster storm commanded premium air time, but the networks eventually dropped the story of the missing aircraft. Nearly a week had passed since the disappearance of Michael's plane, and any hope of finding survivors had faded.

The hurricane's inexorable northerly track paralleled the Mexican coast, placing the eye less than eight hundred miles southwest of Acapulco.

Something had gone terribly wrong with the Department of Weather's advanced warning system prior to landfall, and scientists back at the National Hurricane Center began to take the heat. The incident had also strained diplomatic relations between Colombia and the United States. Some even suggested the U.S. had intentionally let the storm slip through their forecasting net as a sort of atonement for Colombia's ineffective drug interdiction efforts.

Erik paced inside the trailer. If he could just reach Heather, he might be able to persuade her to investigate the matter, perhaps convince her to focus that high-powered journalistic curiosity on the circumstances surrounding the Colombian disaster. He combed the hair back on his head with open fingers and grabbed his keys. It was time to pay Heather Conroy another visit.

⑥

Exiting the 405 Freeway at Wilshire, Erik gazed across the sea of city lights, the sprawl and traffic of L.A. High above the boulevard he saw a marquee advertising Ocean Broadcasting.

He wheeled his Saab around back and parked in the only spot he could find, a ten-minute green-zone beside an overflowing dumpster. Adjacent to the broadcasting center was a five-story parking garage. Erik raised the collar of his coat and moved past the ticket kiosk where a sign read TENANTS ONLY!

Staying near the perimeter wall, he made his way up the concrete ramp. By the time he reached the third floor, there was still no sign of Heather's car. Suddenly, a security guard in a white Hyundai squealed around the corner, making his rounds. Erik froze in the shadows and waited for the guard to pass.

Halfway between the third and fourth floors he spotted a black BMW with Florida plates, Heather's Beemer—tennis racket on the back seat, change of clothes on a hanger.

Several minutes passed before he heard the elevator chime and the sound of people bidding each other goodnight. The voices trailed off in the darkness, and he heard the telltale click of heels on concrete. Peering around a column, he watched her approach. As she got close, he stepped out from the shadows.

"Jeez!" she said, grabbing her chest. "You scared the crap out of me."

"It's good to see you, too," he said, feeling his face rise into a smile.

Clutching her key like a weapon, she said, "I heard you were out here. Sorry about your job."

"Relax," he said, shuffling closer. "I just want to talk."

"You don't need to skulk around like this. You should have phoned."

"I guess congratulations are in order," he said. "Looks like you got everything you wanted."

"And you?"

"I get by," he said.

"I thought you'd be in Central America by now."

"Why? The storm's gonna be here soon enough."

"That's ridiculous," she said. "They don't have hurricanes in California."

"Not yet, but that's not what I came here to talk to you about." He inched closer. "I was set up."

"Really?" she said. "By whom?"

"Probably the same people that blacked out our systems and covered up the hurricane's tracks."

"Do you know how crazy that sounds, all this conspiratorial nonsense? If you're not careful, people are going to start talking behind your back."

"Let them talk, what happened in Colombia was no accident. Someone shut down those satellite feeds."

"Who'd do something like that?"

"You might start by asking Bobby Ocean a few questions."

"That should do wonders for my career," she said, easing her key into the Beemer's lock.

For an instant their eyes met, and he wanted to draw her close. She looked like she might be thinking the same thing, but he couldn't be sure.

They began talking at precisely the same moment, then stopped to share a momentary laugh. She blushed in the low light of the garage.

"What happened to that investigative reporter I used to know?"

"Tell you what...I have to pick up my daughter, but I'll think about what you said. If you make any discoveries, anything concrete, let me know."

"How do I reach you?"

She scribbled her direct line onto the back of a card and slipped it into his hand. An instant later, she slid behind the wheel and revved the engine.

Erik started slowly down the ramp. He glanced over his shoulder for one last look, but the BMW was gone.

CHAPTER 33

Storm track

The storm sliced to leeward, passing not so neatly between Cabo San Lucas and the Revillagigedo Islands, the westernmost point in territorial Mexico. Sustained winds exceeded one-hundred-ninety miles per hour, and huge surf was expected as far north as California.

A hurricane watch had been called along the Pacific coast of Baja, and anyone without a damn good reason for being there was advised to avoid the area altogether.

The Labor Day holiday was fast approaching. Erik kept up his daily tracking with the discipline of a saint, recording the hurricane's every move. The only other eastern Pacific storm ever to come close to being as dangerous was Linda back in 1997, only she hadn't killed anyone.

He punched the San Diego Weather Service's number into his cell phone, and Otto Winderman answered on the first ring.

Erik leaned back in his chair. "Have you seen the latest?"

"Looks like we're in the clear."

"You'd better have another look."

"Why assume the worst," Otto said. "Odds are the hurricane will spin harmlessly out to sea."

"You haven't been tracking the sea temps. I have, and I'll tell you what, this storm's trouble sure as rain. I'm simply suggesting you take some precautionary steps, maybe hold a news conference and encourage preparedness."

"With all due respect, Erik, you're single and unemployed. I've got a family to support and responsibilities. I can't afford to go off half-cocked, whipping people into a frenzy."

"What if you're forced to evacuate? A big storm like this could turn the L.A. basin into undersea parking—there's a reason they call it the basin, you know."

Otto remained silent.

"What about Catalina?" Erik went on. "Come Labor Day you could have fifteen thousand people out there, and no way to get them back in a hurry. Remember Galveston? They lost nine thousand. Takes a lot of boats to evacuate an island the size of Catalina."

"I'll see what I can do."

Satisfied, Erik cradled the receiver and returned to work.

@

Early the following morning the Weather Service office was besieged with reporters. Word had somehow leaked out that the hurricane was headed for U.S. soil. Otto spent the morning trying to fend off the press and swearing at Erik under his breath.

@

Erik kept a low profile, choosing to assist via a remote computer link-up from the trailer in Huntington Beach. He had predicted a hurricane in the unseasonably warm seas off the Southern California coast, and for once he wished his forecast was flawed.

The Hurricane Center in Miami sent along two of its own people to investigate, Tai Jeffers and Professor Yoshida.

It had been several days since the killer storm had emerged in the Pacific. At first, it appeared the hurricane would pass harmlessly into oblivion.

Late at night in a far-off corner of the Pacific, the hurricane did the improbable. It took a gentle arc beyond Guadalupe Island and passed thirty degrees north with ease, headed straight for Southern California.

CHAPTER 34

On target

Erik heard the news—all the networks were carrying it. While the governor's office contemplated the impending state of emergency, local authorities prepared to evacuate low-lying coastal areas and the channel islands.

The deck outside the travel trailer creaked before Erik heard the knocking. He pushed himself away from his laptop and got up to answer the door.

Otto's large frame filled the doorway. "Are you the one who put those newshounds on me? I know it was you, so you might as well fess up."

"It wasn't me," Erik said with a smile, thinking of Yoshida back at the Center.

Grateful Erik hadn't put the dogs on him, Otto's expression began to change. "I'm on my way to the Coast Guard OPS Center. If you feel like getting in the middle of things, I could use the company."

He didn't have to ask twice. Erik grabbed his sweatshirt and followed him toward a government-issue sedan.

"They're evacuating Catalina, like you advised."

"About time," Erik said.

Otto unlocked the door. "Here's your chance to look good. The governor's gonna be there. He wants everyone off Catalina...yesterday. Doesn't want another Galveston on his hands, can't say I blame him."

Erik switched on his hand-held weather radio. A small craft advisory had been called over the inner and outer waters, and the marine report warned of heavy weather. Nasty conditions for all but the largest vessels: twenty-foot seas over the inner waters, with bigger seas brewing on the outside.

@

Forty-five minutes later, they crossed an old iron bridge into L.A. harbor and turned onto Pico Boulevard. There was no mistaking the Coast Guard OPS Center—the streets were choked with every kind of news and emergency vehicle imaginable.

"I'll catch up with you," Otto said, heading in the direction of a mobile command center bearing a NOAA insignia.

Erik headed for an emergency meeting, already underway. Tai flashed a smile and joined him near the edge of the room. Yoshida followed a moment later.

"What are you doing here?" Erik asked.

"We're on our way to Catalina," she said. "The department needs people on the ground to observe the hurricane's landfall firsthand."

"That's absurd, winds in the eyewall are gusting over two hundred. I've been on that island. Trust me, it's the last place you want to be during a CAT 5 hurricane."

A Coast Guard officer with plenty of stripes angled across the room, a real spit and polish type.

"I told her to stay behind," Yoshida complained. "But me? I'm expendable, an old man without a family, without anyone."

Tai shook her head. "And what kind of a future do I have with Michael gone?"

"I won't allow it," Erik insisted. "I'm the one who should be going."

"I'm afraid you won't be going anywhere near that island," said the Coast Guard officer. "My orders are explicit—oversee the immediate evacuation of all persons from Catalina using every available resource, including the four commercial operators who currently provide transportation to the island. And that's exactly what I'm doing."

"You're putting my associates at extreme risk, why?"

The officer disregarded Erik's question. "We are to rendezvous at The Mole where boarding will commence. Once Catalina's been successfully evacuated, we'll accompany Drs. Yoshida and Jeffers to the casino building where the collection of storm data will commence."

Erik glanced over at Tai.

"The order came directly from the Department of Weather," she said, "from Ocean himself."

"Now if you don't mind," the officer interrupted, "my car's waiting outside."

Tai hoisted a duffel bag over her shoulder and grazed Erik's arm on her way to the door. Yoshida followed, a nervous expression in his eyes.

As he watched his friends exit the OPS Center, Erik worried about the mission for which they had been called to serve. He reached the curb a few moments later, just as the Coast Guard sedan squealed around the corner.

CHAPTER 35

Evacuation

The following afternoon Erik discovered a message too curious to resist on his answering machine, a personal invitation from Robert Ocean, along with explicit directions to his beach house on prestigious Harbor Island.

Shortly after the official hurricane warning went out, a single Huntington Beach Police cruiser showed up at the trailer park. The black-and-white made a couple of passes, its P.A. system repeating the same evacuation order again and again.

In less than twenty minutes Erik had the Saab packed to the headliner. He sat in the front seat with an Orange County map book open in his lap, watching an endless procession of cars inch north toward safety.

Instead, Erik turned south in the direction of Harbor Island and the storm. Outside the window, waves pounded the shoreline, threatening Surf Town USA's world-renowned pier. Spent breakers surged up the beach, overturning lifeguard towers and spilling into an area that had once been a parking lot.

Beneath the spreading feeder clouds, flocks of sea birds sailed toward shore, a sign of deteriorating weather. If not for his two stranded friends and Ocean's intriguing invitation, he would have driven a hundred miles inland.

Catalina's familiar silhouette rose against the horizon. Near the pier, a handful of die-hard surfers paddled out to brave the giant surf. Through the Saab's open window came the din of car horns and the wail of sirens. Erik swung the wheel to dodge a pedestrian chancing to cross the highway.

Soon the hurricane would roll ashore, shredding everything in its path, a hard-hitting disaster the likes of which no one up or down the California coast had ever endured.

Sheets of plywood were hurriedly fitted over shop windows, and sandbags were stacked along the seaward side of the highway. The coastal communities were linked together by the fate of their proximity.

Just north of Newport Beach the traffic slowed to a stop near a low-slung bridge. The rising surf washed over the viaduct, and drivers hesitated to cross. The sound of horns and yelling rose above the wind.

Erik spotted a breach in the traffic and steered the Saab around a stalled car and back into traffic. Water thrummed against the floorboard as he hastened over the bridge.

Soon, the seaside community would come eye to eye with the worst disaster nature could dish out, a Category 5 hurricane. The sky resembled a kaleidoscope—clouds converging, rushing toward the center, fueling the atmospheric machine. More water rushed over the roadbed, and he struggled with the wheel.

The unmistakable wail of Civil Defense sirens, unused since the cold war days, echoed up and down the coast. He spun the radio dial until he found NOAA's official Weather Radio broadcast.

Back at the Hurricane Center, he'd worked closely with broadcasters, assisting with links to Weather Radio's Specific Area Message Encoding or SAME. For better or worse, all such communications were now being transmitted over the airways care of Ocean Broadcasting, Incorporated.

A group of thrill seekers climbed out on a jetty for a closer look at the surf. Erik couldn't believe his eyes. He swung toward the curb and jumped out of his car to warn them. Motioning with his hand, he beckoned the group toward shore. They remained on the jetty, transfixed by the rapture of the waves.

A patrol boat shot through the surf. One of the lifeguards aboard hollered something though his bullhorn and pointed toward the beach. Just then, the surf began to run out and the boat slued sideways.

Erik shuffled closer for a better look as the panicked thrill seekers turned toward shore. More water ran out, the kind of extraordinary motion the sea goes through while piling up on itself. The lifeguard rescue boat turned offshore and flew out of the surf as it made for deeper water.

The thrill seekers were pointing, too, and Erik soon discovered why. An enormous wave rose out of the sea, easily twice the size of the previous set. Amazement turned to panic as the wave continued to grow, twenty feet tall if it measured an inch.

The rogue wave showed its dark underbelly, and Erik heard the sound of screaming. The thrill seekers tripped over each other as they shouldered their way toward shore.

There was nothing anyone could do but watch. The wave rumbled toward shore, swallowing everything in its path.

When the water finally subsided, not a soul appeared in the roiling foam. Then a head and a hand, then more. Soon, Erik counted six people in all, struggling in the surf.

An orange and white Coast Guard helicopter sailed in from the north with a rescue swimmer perched in its open door. Lifeguards made their way through the foam, towing torpedo-shaped rescue buoys.

The scene reminded Erik of the nightmarish wave he'd spent a lifetime trying to forget. He returned to his car, relieved that the fates of the hapless thrill seekers rested in the hands of rescuers.

In less than twenty-four hours the California coast would experience the hurricane's unrestrained fury. Erik pulled from the curb and thought about his friends. By now, they were probably hunkered down, preparing for the worst.

The notion of a hurricane party held at ground-zero was bizarre at best. Still, he had every intention of attending.

The success of any truly memorable storm soiree depended on interesting guests, a well-stocked bar and at least one chance in two of coming out alive. Ocean was one of the few people capable of ordering an emergency rescue, and Erik was determined to make his appeal.

A spin of the radio dial produced mostly static, punctuated by a repetitious Civil Defense message, warning of high winds and deadly tides. He knew the drill.

⊚

The surf grew larger by the minute, and more rain began to fall. Erik gazed out to sea. Catalina offered little in the way of hurricane-proof shelter, and he wondered why the authorities had failed to attempt a rescue, let alone why they'd ordered Tai and Yoshida out there in the first place. He had tried his best to discourage his friends, but each had their reasons for going.

Erik clung to his shield, a half-baked weather theory at best. He punched some swamp pop into the cassette player and cranked up the volume, watching miles of parked cars jam every road, street, highway, boulevard and freeway radiating away from the coast. A few brave souls who'd been waiting out the storm apparently changed their minds and left with all they could carry.

Despite the driving rain, Erik felt strangely calm. Somewhere out there loomed an even larger wave, the immense wave that had taken his father and Samuelson. In the cold sweat of his nightmares the wave had appeared quite green. The blackish-green of some awful, barnacle-scarred leviathan come to the surface to smell the sweet scent of land.

Intent upon keeping his appointment, he pressed on, squinting through the rain and hoping the way was clear. In case the road leading to ultra-exclusive Harbor Island happened to be closed or guarded, he had a pass, the laminated Department of Weather ID card he kept buried in his wallet.

Fit, plumb and freshly painted, a majestic paddle-wheeler graced a protected bay on the seaward side of the highway. Erik stared toward the stormy horizon, then back at the boat. The old girl appeared to be a long way from her muddy Mississippi roots. It was a pity she'd never survive the night.

CHAPTER 36

Hurricane party

Erik hung an immediate right past the paddle-wheeler and sloshed through a neighborhood of boarded-up villas on his way to Harbor Island. He passed beyond a formidable iron gate stalled in the open position and crossed a timeworn concrete bridge.

He idled down a cobblestone court where island estates sprawled into deep bay-front lots. Up ahead, a half-dozen colorful balloons tugged at a swaying ginkgo tree.

The house had been fashioned from quarried gray stone, no doubt the remains of some unfortunate dismantled castle or fortress. Beneath the ginkgo tree stood Bobby Ocean, dressed in a fashionable black overcoat. Beside him, a platinum Bentley Arnage.

He tossed a busted umbrella to the wind and cupped his hands against his mouth. "I see you found my little beach house."

"Hard to miss," Erik said, staring up at the edifice.

Atop the roof, a copper weathervane creaked in the backing wind.

"I'd like to introduce you to some people," Ocean said, starting for the house. "And you needn't bother with the keys, your car's perfectly safe on the island."

Erik studied the fast-moving storm clouds and had his doubts. Nevertheless, he set the parking brake, stepped into the rain and followed the Weather Czar toward an immense wooden door.

"What can I get you?" Ocean said, moving past the threshold.

"Soda's fine."

"Ever attended a hurricane party before?"

Before Erik could answer, an overweight chef burst through a swinging door and tore off his apron. He swore something in French and stormed toward his car without looking back.

"Andre's a little nervous about the weather," said a blond man with a thick accent.

A moment later, a second man sporting a cook's apron leaned through the open doorway. "Bon appetit."

Erik studied the men, and then it hit him—the visiting entourage back in Miami.

Ocean returned with an ice-filled tumbler, fizzing with soda. "I'm afraid it's nearly impossible to find quality help these days."

Erik couldn't blame the chef for leaving. For a moment, he even considered joining him, all the way out to the Nevada border if necessary. The moment passed, and he made the irrevocable decision to stay. After all, he'd come to Harbor Island to arrange the rescue of his friends.

"Someone needs to get those forecasters off Catalina Island," he blurted.

"Perhaps you can tell us all about it," Ocean said, "later, after dinner."

While on the subject of his discontent, Erik considered bringing up a few other issues with the Weather Czar. He just couldn't shake the suspicion that someone, somewhere, had caused the communication breakdowns plaguing the nation—probably the same people who wanted him gone.

Ocean raised his glass in a toast. "A salute to the storm—may we all see the light of day."

Crystal came together in the flickering light, and Ocean turned to Erik. "Allow me to introduce the future deputy assistant secretary of the Department of Weather, Gustav Bruner."

"Cheers," Bruner said, clinking his glass against Erik's.

"And this," he said, wrapping his arm around his attorney's narrow shoulders, "is Karl Spicer, my trusted legal advisor."

"Charmed," Spicer said, spearing a drunk olive from the

bottom of his glass.

Erik observed the proceedings, the way Ocean kept glancing through the prism-cut window in the direction of the bridge.

Spicer helped himself to an hors d'oeuvre. "So, you're the disaster guy?"

"I guess you could say that."

"Dr. Reynard's been on leave, but we hope to change all that, don't we, Doctor?"

"I'd like my job back, if that's what you're driving at."

"All in good time," Ocean said, leading him down a stone hallway. "Permit me to show you around."

What the house lacked in size, it more than made up for in quality. Even the head looked gold-plated.

"I hope your insurance is paid up," Erik said. "If the storm comes ashore as predicted, this entire island will be twenty feet underwater."

"Pity," Ocean said, running his hand down an ancient Greek column.

He smiled and turned a cool ear to the gathering blow, like a person with a contingency plan. If, indeed, he had such a plan, he hadn't taken the time to share its details.

Outside, the wind began to crank. Ocean closed the shutters and put away an unused brandy snifter.

"Dinner is served," Spicer called from the doorway.

After a meal of rare lamb, wild rice and a delightful Andalouse compote, Erik pardoned himself and followed the sound of strings emanating from the parlor. Ocean joined him a minute later, extending a cigar.

"No thanks," Erik said.

"Pity, they're Cubans. Sure you won't reconsider?"

"Not tonight."

Tinkling notes resonated around the room as the wind found its way through a partially opened window. Ocean lit his cigar and lifted an instrument from the windowsill. It consisted of a flat wooden sound box with two holes in the top and strings that ran lengthwise.

Ocean closed the window. "It's an aeolian harp. It makes music when wind passes over the strings."

A moment later they were joined by Gustav Bruner and Karl Spicer.

Ocean turned the harp in his hands. "There's a term for the physics involved, but I'm afraid it escapes me."

"Sympathetic vibration," Erik said.

Ocean handed the instrument to Erik. "I'd forgotten there's a scientist among us."

Erik balanced the harp in his hands and blew lightly across the strings. Suddenly, the lights flickered, and the harp was drowned out by the howling wind. Ocean shut the drapes, but not before Erik had a lingering look outside. A long gray dock projected from the rear of the property, with a storage box and light at the end. Moored to the dock was a sleek offshore racing boat.

"About the rescue attempt," Erik said, glancing nervously at his watch.

"Over espresso," Ocean insisted, leading the group back to the dining room.

Erik followed the others and took his seat. Out in the kitchen he heard the sound of escaping steam. A few minutes later, Ocean appeared with a serving tray and four porcelain cups.

"Did you know Colombia's the western hemisphere's leading coffee producer?"

"Eleven percent of the world's total," said Erik.

"Actually," Ocean said, "it's twelve percent. The world's coffee prices rest in the hands of a few key growers. It's all about supply."

"Probably more profitable than the cocaine trade," Erik said. "Coffee prices must've rocketed in the wake of the hurricane. Now, about my friends?"

"Perhaps we should let them get on with the business of observing."

"If you don't approve a rescue mission, right now, you'll be signing their death warrants."

Ocean slid a cup and saucer in Erik's direction. "I'm afraid a rescue's out of the question."

"You have to do something, tonight, before the hurricane

makes landfall."

"Relax," Ocean said, "enjoy your espresso. I'm sure they'll manage."

"Manage?" he snapped. "Do you have any appreciation for the power of a Category 5 hurricane?"

Ocean reached into his vest pocket for a long cigar. "Tell me, Doctor, exactly how much do you know about commodities?"

Erik's heart began to race. The espresso, the questions about Colombia, the satellite blackouts—everything began to make sense.

Bruner reached inside his coat and withdrew a very real gun.

Erik contemplated diving headlong through a pair of French doors leading to the garden but, judging from Bruner's deft handling of the gun, he doubted he'd get to a standing position, let alone through the glass.

Spicer rose slowly from his chair. "What's going on, Robert?"

"Well, Counselor, we can't just let the good doctor walk out of here, now, can we?"

Erik said, "I don't know what you're up to, and I don't really care. I only came here to negotiate my friends' rescue."

"It's nothing personal," Ocean said, his head articulating slowly on his shoulders. "Actually, I admire your steadiness under fire."

Bruner twisted a silencer onto the muzzle of his gun and leveled the weapon at Erik's chest.

"Give the gun to Spicer," Ocean said. "Let him finish it. We'll reconfirm Mr. Spicer's commitment and silence the good doctor, all with a single bullet"

Bruner's eyes came alive. He smiled and slid the Heckler & Koch semiautomatic across the polished table.

Spicer took one look at the gun and nervously backed away. "For God's sake, man, we can't kill him."

"We?" Ocean said.

Bruner produced a coil of rope and a pocketknife and slid them in front of Spicer. Erik recognized the knife at once, the same Boy Scout knife his father had given him, missing from his desk drawer since the day he left the Hurricane Center.

Ocean said, "You're a yachtsman, tie him up."

The attorney downed the last of his brandy and retrieved the rope with a shaky hand. "I'm afraid we've stooped to the flagitious."

Erik locked eyes with the Weather Czar. "Bobby Ocean, isn't that what they used to call you? You've come a long ways from reporting the weather on the evening news."

"You might show some respect," Ocean said, honing his cigar ash inside an empty snifter. "Look at you, one foot out of the swamp, with your dirty rice and barefoot ways. They'd probably never seen the likes of you before at MIT." He puffed the Cuban back to life.

A cherry ripened at the end of the cigar, and Erik hoped it wasn't intended for his flesh. "How'd you do it, all those agencies, the technology, QuikSCAT, JPL, NASA?"

"Helps to have friends in high places. And regarding the death toll in Colombia, there's no guarantee it would have been any lower, even with an advanced warning. Those villagers were doomed from the start."

"You killed them, you sick sonofabitch."

"Natural disasters happen all the time," Ocean said with indifference. "Earthquakes in Central Asia routinely kill thousands."

"With earthquakes, there's no advance warning. But you knew about the storm. You knew and somehow managed to withhold vital information until it was too late."

"A little flooding in the central mountains of Colombia will hardly rouse world suspicion. Besides, I'm sure the State Department was only too happy to look the other way when the hurricane battered the headquarters of the cocaine cartel."

"Don't be so sure."

"Communications occasionally get interrupted. You're a scientist, surely you know that."

Erik glared. "Want to know what did it for me? Redundant systems collapsing in the face of the worst hurricane on record, it just didn't add up. Do what you want with me, but others will know. They'll figure out how you manipulated those systems and track you down. I left a tape, and it tells everything—about the ransacking of Samuelson's trailer, the disappearance of his research journals, the satellite blackouts, everything."

"We both know there aren't any tapes. Besides, the hurricane will take care of whatever evidence you may have been foolish enough to leave behind at that broken down trailer you call home."

Erik wondered how long he'd been under surveillance and struggled against his restraints. Perhaps they'd implicate themselves by fleeing to avoid prosecution.

Ocean lifted the H&K semiautomatic and slid it back to Bruner. "Who else knows about this little theory of yours?"

Erik hesitated a moment too long, and the gun came down hard.

"My jet's standing by at John Wayne Airport with the best avionics money can buy. Six thousand miles could put a lot of distance between you and the storm."

"No, thanks. You might get airborne, but you'll be looking over your shoulder for the rest of your life, hunted and on the run."

Erik felt a warm drop of blood drip down his cheek. On the brink of passing out, he somehow managed to keep the store lit, the pain his only link to consciousness. After several seconds, he opened his eyes and turned his stare on Ocean.

"Those satellite blackouts will be investigated," he mumbled. "They'll never jell with Deevers, suspicious sonofabitch will be all over it like a pit bull. He won't stop until he figures it out."

"Oh, everything will add up, all right. Bruner's seen to that."

The unsolicited compliment earned a proud smile from Ocean's accomplice.

"And don't be so sure about Deevers. He's the quintessential bureaucrat, spends his time counting the number of days until retirement. If you came here to confirm your suspicions, congratulations. But if you came here out of some pathetic sense of justice, I'm afraid you're out of luck. Pity, I could have used someone like you. Tell me who you've spoken to about this, and I promise to make this quick."

Bruner withdrew a small metal case from inside his coat and moved closer. Inside the case was a hypodermic and two small ampoules. He punctured one of the ampoules and filled the syringe.

"Where'd you get him?" Erik sneered. "Psychos To Go?"

"Shut your face," Bruner said, throwing him a backhand.

The pain coursed down Erik's jaw like molten lead.

Ocean settled into his chair. "I'd be careful if I were you. He once sliced a man's ear clean off and fed it to jackals, belongs to a group that makes the Broederbond look like a bunch of choir boys. They know how to deal with troublemakers back in South Africa. People have a way of simply disappearing."

Erik kept his eyes fixed on the Weather Czar.

"A moment ago, you said that others would know. You said they would investigate. What others?"

Erik managed a low-grade smile despite his swollen lip.

"Just as I thought. There is no one else, no one except your doomed comrades. It's a pity the Coast Guard had to abandon its rescue attempt. I'm afraid I had no other choice." Ocean glanced at his watch. "The hurricane should reach Catalina by daybreak—there won't be a stick left standing."

Erik glanced over at Spicer. "You think the government doesn't know what's going on? Don't kid yourself. Help me out, and I'll tell them you did the right thing in the end."

"Don't listen to him," Ocean warned.

"Your friends delayed the transmission of important storm data just long enough to profit from the escalating coffee prices," Erik said. "They must've made millions, hundreds of millions, maybe. Tell me, how much did they cut you in for?"

Spicer mapped the exits with his eyes. "I knew something like this would happen. Don't you see? It's just like Reynard said."

"Quiet!" Ocean blurted.

"I don't care how well Bruner covered things up. What are the odds against those satellites breaking down before the hurricane made landfall, a billion to one? More?" Spicer's eyes flashed with panic. "Don't you see? Others will know. They'll know, and they'll come with subpoenas and warrants."

Ocean gave a silent command to Bruner, a glance, nothing more. Bruner slammed the hypodermic directly into Spicer's neck. The attorney's eyes rolled back white as the drug entered his bloodstream.

The needle made a mainline entry into his carotid artery,

and a single drop of blood trickled down his neck. He fell to the floor, rolled to his side and convulsed.

"It's an experimental drug, quite impossible to detect," Ocean said, observing Spicer with passing interest. He lifted the pocketknife with a linen napkin and slid it inside Erik's pocket. "I believe this is yours."

Bruner left the room and returned a few moments later dragging a canvas sail bag.

Erik strained unsuccessfully to reach the knife. The hurricane party made perfect sense. When he came to Harbor Island petitioning his friends' rescue, he tumbled unwittingly into Ocean's trap. Fearing he was next, he watched Bruner work Spicer into the canvas sail bag.

The fact they bothered with the drug at all was probably a good thing. They could have simply shot them both and been done with it. Escaping the hurricane's onslaught would be the tricky part. His death may have been imminent, but it wasn't necessarily immediate.

Beyond the French doors, clouds converged. Feeder bands sailed toward the hurricane's center like water down a thirsty drain.

Erik yawned to equalize the falling pressure—the barometer was dropping fast. The wind gusting across the bay neared hurricane strength. He could hear it.

Ocean turned his attention toward the sea. "The storm's getting closer."

Bruner cinched the canvas bag and parked it near the door.

"Sorry about the rope, but I'm afraid it was necessary. It simply wouldn't do to have you escape. Mr. Bruner will be removing your restraints soon enough."

Erik stared across the bay at the rising tide. At best, the chair in which he sat was a mere six feet above sea level. The hurricane was capable of producing a devastating storm surge, and soon the entire island would be underwater.

Bruner unlatched the French doors and blocked them open with a pair of Chinese vases. He took hold of the man-sized bag and began to pull, over the threshold and down the gangway toward the dock.

He returned a few minutes later, breathing hard.

Disposing of Spicer had apparently taxed him. He toyed with the hypodermic case and withdrew the remaining ampoule.

Outside, a trash can careened across the yard.

"Pity you're such a Boy Scout," Ocean said. "Things might have worked out differently."

Realizing he and Spicer were about to be exposed to the unprotected fury of the storm, Erik experienced a moment of pure dread. He tried to free himself, but it was no use—the knots held fast.

"Finish it," Ocean said. "We're running late."

Bruner held the syringe up to the flickering light while a tree limb banged against the glass. He depleted the ampoule and pressed the plunger, dislodging a cluster of stubborn bubbles.

Without warning, the bay-front window exploded. Ignoring the shards, Bruner methodically scrubbed Erik's arm. Not for the sake of hygiene, he thought, but to tease a suitable vein into view.

Erik refused to oblige him. But his vasculature could hide no longer, and a telltale blue vein slowly revealed itself.

He'd never forget the expression on Bruner's face, like a crow peering in on a hatchling. He probed at the vein with analytic curiosity, jabbing and missing several times before going mainline. The tissue began to purple as a plum-sized hematoma bloomed beneath the skin.

"There you are," he said, "such a nice fat vein."

The guy practiced medicine with a level of creepiness uniquely his own, taking several times as long as the most ham-handed nurse.

Erik clung to sobriety, trying to prevent the drug from entering his brain.

The drug's effect was immediate and irresistible, like a strange new gravity. He felt as though he'd been scooped up by an enormous wave and rolled end over end into a watery black hole. A moment later, there was nothing.

CHAPTER 37

Not cleared for takeoff

Cracks began to appear in Robert Ocean's stoic exterior despite careful planning and execution. He and Bruner had exercised the utmost discretion in their dealings—still, he couldn't seem to shake Reynard's warning.

The rafters bucked, and a section of the roof peeled away. It was high time to get moving.

Ocean started for the door. "Take the Saab and follow me."

"What about the Hummer?" Bruner said.

"One trip to the Grand Caymans and you can buy all the cars you want."

A plan was hatched whereby Erik's car would be left at a low stretch of beach near the pier. The storm would take care of the rest. It was a short trip to the drop site, down coastal roads littered with debris. Waves spilled over a sea wall constructed of hastily stacked sandbags, and green water surged down the street.

Bruner tailed Robert Ocean's Bentley through the devastation before turning into a beachfront parking lot. He jumped from the moving car and watched it idle toward the surf.

The Bentley peeled away before Bruner could get the door shut. "Are you sure we can get airborne in this storm?"

"I have no intention of abandoning my plane," Ocean said over the turbo's whine. "It's just a little farther."

A pair of emergency vehicles shot past them in the opposite direction, down the boulevard with their red lights flashing, sirens barely distinguishable above the wind.

The Bentley rocketed up MacArthur. The storm was right behind them, roaring toward the coast like a dragon. Light standards swayed and street signs flapped in the wind. Ocean ran a flashing red signal and sped into the airport at sixty plus. Up ahead, the Gulfstream beckoned, strobe lights flashing through the rain.

"We'll never get clearance to take off in this," Bruner said, eyeing the stormy sky. "Maybe we should drive out of here while there's still time."

Ocean screeched to a stop. "Just get aboard the plane. This time tomorrow, we'll be visiting our money."

The pilot rose from behind the controls. "The hurricane's got everyone grounded."

Ocean considered the weather over his shoulder. Surely the Gulfstream's legendary thrust would be sufficient to get them safely above the storm clouds. He pushed past the pilot and gazed at the cluster of instruments.

"Are you fueled up?"

The pilot nodded.

"Good, shut the door and prepare for takeoff."

"I can't do that," he said. "I'll lose my certification."

Bruner stepped between them, looking irritated.

"This is all the certification you need," he said, shoving his gun in the pilot's face. "Get moving!"

CHAPTER 38

Rude awakening

Perhaps it was the bay water streaming up through the floor that roused him, maybe it was the wind—Erik wasn't sure. He blinked his eyelids and shivered, wondering where in the hell he was.

The tomb in which he found himself was small and dark. He reached up and pushed, but the ceiling remained secure. Everywhere, the sound of wind and rising water. He worked his hands down to his sides and pressed outward, but the walls wouldn't budge. His mind flashed on the evening's events. He remembered seeing the dockside storage box earlier, near the end of a long gray dock.

Something smashed against the side of his tomb, and his world began to list. The events of the previous evening came creeping back. Unease turned to dread as he calculated his limited prospects for survival.

The shrinking airspace smelled of oily rags, boat wax and fuel. Erik hacked and coughed, trying to expel the noxious air from his lungs. Outside, the wind shrieked. His fingers mapped the ceiling of his cell when a pain shot up his arm, the drug's point of entry. Bruner had given him something potent, some sort of synthetic narcotic—he'd heard of such things.

The saltwater stung his rope-burned wrists. The restraints were gone, now. Gone, too, were Bruner and Bobby Ocean.

The air around him shrank as the water level rose. Pushing

upward, he felt something roll beneath him. Suddenly, the prospect of drowning, of becoming a statistic, began to sink in.

For a moment he imagined being back with his father, poling around the Louisiana swamp of his dreams, the wind backing around them like a serpent through the trees.

His fingertips found a pair of screw heads along the upper edge of his cell, hard and metallic, unmistakable. Drawing his thumb across the head of the first screw, he felt his nail catch in the telltale groove.

His right hand found the folding Boy Scout knife inside his pocket. He worked it slowly toward his chest, careful not to drop it, searching for the screwdriver blade.

A quarter turn of the screw, then a half turn, the fastener barely backing. The fiberglass had swollen over the years, causing the screw to cinch.

His progress was slow. The water continued to rise. Without warning, the screw fell from the rusty hinge plate and hit him squarely in the face. He blinked, trying to work the irritating grit out of his eyes.

Above the wind he heard something else, the unmistakable sound of footsteps racing down the dock. In desperation, he banged against the lid. The footsteps drew closer.

"Help!" he cried. "I'm in here."

His voice was hoarse and weak, his vocal chords barely emerging from the paralysis of deep sedation. He heard the sound of hands working furiously at the latch, and felt a man-sized lump roll beneath him. "Get me out of here."

At last, the dockside storage box creaked open. Overhead, a sodium vapor lamp flickered through the sea mist, framing Heather in an aura. "Oh my God, Erik? You don't look so good."

He tried to stand, but his legs were numb. "It took you long enough to find me."

"Is that the best you can do?" she said, helping him stand. "How about a simple thank you?"

"Sorry."

Heather stared down at her rain-soaked dress and stringy hair. "Guess I missed the party."

Erik struggled for balance. "Thank God you were fashionably late."

"Hardly fashionable," she said, pulling at her clingy dress. "It was bumper to bumper, all the way from Santa Monica. Took me five long hours to get here."

"I hate to think what might have happened if you'd been on time." The wind gusted as the storm loomed closer. "Did you get my letter?"

She nodded.

"Where's Ocean and that sonofabitch Bruner?"

"Gone," she said, brushing the hair out of her face. "Everyone's gone. I hiked in here, had to climb an iron gate to get past the bridge."

The gusting wind toppled a nearby tree.

"Where's your car?"

"It's stranded out on the highway, flooded. All of Newport's deserted. The police barely let me through. They tried to confiscate my press pass and told me I had no business in an evacuated area."

He stepped unsteadily from the dockside box, feeling the wind against his face. "Where's your daughter?"

"Back in Florida with my parents. It's safer there."

She backed across the partially submerged dock, her jaw quivering.

"What is it?"

"There," she said, pointing a shaky finger at the dockside box. "My God, is that what I think it is?"

Erik stared into the submerged face, puffy and grayish-white, eyes fixed as if staring from some distant world. A custom toupee had floated off the dead man's head, suspended like a hairy jellyfish. He nudged the body with the toe of his shoe and watched it bob easily back and forth.

"Don't touch it," she said.

"I need to be sure."

"He's dead."

Erik hadn't seen too many stiffs in his life, but judging from the depth of the water he was quite certain Spicer was dead, unless he had learned to breath like a fish.

"Who is it?"

"Karl Spicer, Ocean's legal counsel, his ex-legal counsel. They had a little falling out."

Erik contemplated Spicer's exact cause of death—perhaps a reaction to the drug, or hypothermia, or damage to his carotid artery. Perhaps he'd gone into shock or suffered a heart attack. Or, maybe, the drug had reacted with the alcohol in his system. Unlike Spicer, Erik had been sober at the time of his injection. These were questions a medical examiner would have to answer, provided the remains could be found for a proper autopsy.

"What should we do with him?" Heather asked.

Erik watched the corpse float lifelessly inside the dockside storage box and slammed the lid. "Forget it, we've got enough to worry about."

Soon, the coast would be pummeled by hurricane force winds. People and trees gone. Buildings flattened. The monster storm was capable of producing flooding the likes of which California had never known.

Erik took Heather by the hand and led her toward the ramp. By morning, the worst of the storm, the devastating eye-wall, was due to come ashore.

"If Ocean had had his way, two bloated bodies, mine and Spicer's, would have been found by cadaver dogs weeks after the storm."

"That's an awful thought."

"Brilliant actually. Who would have suspected foul play? Just another statistic with the storm singularly to blame."

The wind howled, and Heather stared at him with a pleading look. "You've got to do something about the storm."

"Who do I look like, god of the winds?"

She ducked in close, and he could feel the warmth of her lips against his cheek. Perhaps if they made it out alive, he'd get a second chance with her. It was reason enough to survive the night.

A strong gust of wind caused Heather to steady herself on the railing leading up the dock ramp. "I've been working on an investigative piece," she hollered above the blow. "I may have to find another job once the story airs, it doesn't reflect too kindly on Robert Ocean and company."

"That's my girl."

"You may have figured out who shut down those satellites," she said, sounding quite proud of herself, "but I figured out why."

"Really?"

"Yes, really," she said, stopping halfway up the ramp.

"Does it have anything to do with Ocean's attempt to corner the world's coffee market?"

The wind whipped her stringy hair, and Heather went stone quiet for a few moments. "As a matter of fact, it does. And if you already knew that, why didn't you tell me, you shithead?"

"Would you have believed me?"

She sniffed a little, and he thought he saw a tear or two form in the corners of her eyes, although it could have been a result of the irritating wind.

"We're gonna die out here, aren't we?"

"Not if I can help it," he said. "Come on."

Another sound penetrated the stormy sky during the wee hours of the morning—the growl of a low altitude jet, rocketing overhead.

Erik stared in the direction of the fading jet sound. A few moments later, a power failure darkened the bay. A bit of moonlight streamed through the twisting storm clouds as they reached an expansive deck of terra cotta tiles.

Her heel caught between the pavers. "I'm stuck."

Erik couldn't believe his eyes—she was wearing a strappy pair of pumps. "Heels?"

"They're Bruno Maglis. Do you have any idea what these things cost?"

"They won't do you much good now," he said, bending down to liberate her foot. "You're better off barefoot."

He rose with the shoe in hand and removed the busted heel as if uncorking a wine bottle. "Forget it," he said, rearing back to throw. "It's fish food."

He let go the shoe and watched it splash a good twenty yards from shore.

"That was stupid."

"I'll buy you another pair."

"You better believe it, buster," she said, slipping out of the remaining shoe and hobbling along behind him.

They passed a Japanese stone lantern. Beyond the lantern, the wind fractured the serenity of a Zen meditation pool where silver koi darted nervously through the blackness. It seemed a bit New Age for a reptile like Ocean.

Erik led Heather across a half-dozen stone steps dotting the pond and up the opposite shore where a tenacious black pine held on for dear life. Beyond a grove of bamboo stood an oriental-style gate, the only barrier between them and the street.

Erik pushed on the gate and jiggled the handle. "It's stuck."

"That's strange," Heather said. "It opened for me on the way in." She backed away from the gate and delivered a well-placed kick. Wood shattered about the latch, and the gate swung wide open.

"Where'd you learn to do that?" he said, following her through the opening.

"Women's self-defense class. Be a good boy, and you won't get hurt."

The wind cranked up a notch, and the sound of shattering glass echoed from the bay side of the house.

Gone were the balloons and the ginkgo tree they'd been tied to, blown down the street and out to sea. Missing, too, was Erik's Saab and any sign of Bobby Ocean and company.

"Damn those guys, they stole my car."

Suddenly, the weather vane took flight and embedded itself in a neighboring house.

"We've got to get out of here," he said.

Their eyes leveled on the closed garage door at precisely the same moment. Erik strained at the handle, but the door wouldn't budge.

"Follow me," he said, charging back through the busted gate toward the rear of the villa.

Wind-driven waves lumbered restlessly about the bay. Recalling the French doors at the rear of the villa, Erik led her by the hand. He reached through a blown-out pane and opened the latch. Glass crunched underfoot, and he swung around to sweep her up into his arms.

Heather smiled. "I could get used to this."

"It's because of the broken glass," he said, lowering her to the floor.

"Always the romantic," she said, taking him by the hand. "The garage, come on—it's this way."

"How would you know?"

"Can we please go into that some other time?"

They charged through a lightless doorway, down a few steps and found themselves ankle-deep in water. Doubting the competent southern belle needed much help, Erik guided her through the darkness.

The island would soon be twenty feet underwater, and there wasn't much time. Suddenly, he bumped into something, a car from the feel of it, their ticket to survival.

"Do you have a match?" he said.

"I gave up smoking."

"A light...anything, damnit."

"How about my light-up Ocean Broadcasting key fob?"

"Perfect."

The bulb's narrow beam threw a cone of weak light against a jet black Hummer. Erik bellied up to the all-terrain vehicle and let his fingers graze its polished roofline. Probably the same vehicle spotted out on Hunting Island, he figured. Somehow, he wasn't surprised.

"Get in," he said, whipping open the passenger door.

He ran around to the driver's side, slid behind the wheel and inhaled. The Hummer even smelled new. It was beginning to look like they were home free until his hand went for the ignition and came up short.

"Where in the hell's the key?"

With a push of a button, Heather reactivated her light-up key fob. Erik withdrew his pocketknife and went to work on the ignition switch.

She searched above both visors and inside the glove box, nervously popping her gum.

"Must you do that?"

"I'll do whatever I want," she said, blowing a weak bubble.

"I need something metallic," he said. "A bobby pin."

"Where have you been? I don't use those things."

By now, the switch was fully exposed. Heather popped her gum once more, and Erik stared right through her.

"What's the matter?"

"Gum!" he said, snapping his fingers.

She slapped a stick into his palm. "All you had to do is ask."

Erik tore off the foil wrapper and tossed the gum over his shoulder.

"I thought you wanted a piece?"

He held up the foil. "This is what I need."

In less than four seconds, he had the metallic wrapper crimped to the wiring. Blue sparks flashed beneath the dash, and he blew at his smoking fingertips.

"We've got power."

The starter warbled and quit. Erik managed to make a better connection the second time and pumped the accelerator. A little fuel did the trick, and the Hummer's unmistakable rumble filled the garage.

He tried the garage door opener he found pinched to the visor, but the power was dead.

"Fasten your seat belt," he said, shifting the Hummer into reverse.

The garage door exploded on impact. He spun the off-road vehicle around in the rising water and cast a fair-sized wake over the curb.

Trouble loomed up ahead. The same iron gate that had kept the island free of solicitors, criminals and the prying eyes of the public was also a formidable barrier capable of preventing the condemned from leaving. The motor assembly was as devoid of power as the surrounding bay, and the barrier remained impenetrably and resolutely closed.

Erik took a deep breath and gripped the wheel. "Force equals mass times acceleration, it's basic physics. Something's got to give."

Heather covered her eyes. "Just promise me you'll get us back in one piece."

"Hold on," he said.

The hard-charging Hummer rammed through the gate like a Sherman tank, knocking the barrier clean off its hinges.

CHAPTER 39

Storm tide

The Hummer plunged into the water on the other side of the bridge and plowed toward Pacific Coast Highway. Erik spun the wheel, turning north at an unlit intersection and swerving to miss a stranded station wagon.

Heather swung around in her seat and stared through the rear window. "That was close."

"A little too close," Erik said, bringing the Hummer to a stop.

"What are you doing?" she asked.

He stared out at the devastation, thoughts of survival turning like gears inside his head. If his calculations were correct, the storm's eye would pass directly over Catalina by morning. He listened to the unrelenting rain and drummed his fingers on the wheel. Something had to be done to get his friends off the island, and he knew it was up to him.

The idea came to him suddenly, so crazy it just might work. All he needed was a fully fueled WC-130, a highly skilled pilot and up-to-the-minute satellite imagery of the storm. If they could reach the Hurricane Hunters in time, he might be able to convince them to attempt a rescue.

A sheet of plywood suddenly took flight, and a tree limb tumbled down the highway. The worst was yet to come, much worse. So far, the storm had only flirted with the coast.

"We need a map," he said. "See if there's one in the glove

compartment."

Heather tore through a stack of papers and came up with a folded leather satchel. "Voila!" she said, removing a map of the Golden State.

"Look for March Air Force Base. It's east of here, near the town of Riverside."

Heather whipped open the map and went to work.

"The hurricane's been feeding on tropical air for days. It's stronger, now, deadlier than before. NEXRAD pegged winds near the eyewall at better than two-hundred-miles-per-hour. You have any idea what that means?"

She shook her head.

"Bricks become missiles and a sign post could punch through the windshield like an artillery round."

"So what are we doing parked out here, talking about it?"

He hit the accelerator, and the Hummer splashed its way north, through Newport's boarded-up business district where yachts and imported automobiles had once been showcased.

Erik felt Heather's hand in his and turned to face her.

"Tell me we're going to make it," she said.

"Of course we will."

"Thanks for being such a Boy Scout. It's not every guy that knows how to hot-wire a car like a common criminal."

"Nothing common about it," he said.

Heather smiled a fetching smile. Erik thought she'd never looked better, in a shipwreck survivor sort of way. But something still troubled him, and he'd kept quiet about it as long as he could.

"Amazing how you knew your way around Bobby Ocean's beach house."

Rain buried the windows and wind rocked the Hummer. Heather pulled her hand away and stared silently out the side window. "I didn't say I'd never been there."

"It's none of my business, okay? You can do whatever you want."

"Thanks, I will."

A silence weighed in between them like an invisible anvil.

"You don't owe me an explanation," he said.

The windows began to perspire, and he switched on the defroster. It worked better on the glass than it did on Heather.

"So you had a lousy relationship with your mother," she said. "Get over it."

"At least I didn't sleep with my boss to get ahead."

"Sleep with my boss...what makes you think that?"

"You sure seemed to know your way around."

"I happened to attend a meeting there," she said, "for the West Coast Broadcasting Group."

"Oh, really? Let's just forget it, okay?"

"No, let's talk about it," she said. "I insist!"

"I don't want to talk about it."

"That's right, Erik, run when it gets uncomfortable. Why don't you just admit you're jealous?"

Suddenly, a wayward road sign cartwheeled across the street in front of them. "Me, jealous? That's ridiculous."

Heather's eyes suddenly grew large, the pupils shiny black in the dome light. Her face turned slowly toward the sea.

"Quiet," she said, sweeping the hair behind her ear. "Listen."

"What?"

"There," she said, pointing offshore. "I thought I saw something."

Erik rolled down his window for a better look and stared out to sea. His heart leapt upward in his chest as the horizon suddenly rose above the rooftops.

He jammed his foot against the accelerator. "We've got to get out of here."

The storm surge rolled toward the coast like a killer tsunami. Erik steered through the maze of stalled cars and debris, trying to beat the rising water. The entrance to the Newport Freeway lay just ahead. If they reached the onramp in time, they might gain enough elevation to escape the towering wall of water.

"Can't you go any faster?" she pleaded.

He gritted his teeth and felt the tires slip. By the time he realized he'd taken the turn too fast, the Hummer slid to a stop against the guardrail.

"Shit!" he yelled, whipping the Hummer into reverse and back onto the road.

A row of buildings on the seaward side of the highway exploded in foam. The Hummer fishtailed, and Erik turned into the skid, keeping his foot to the floor, watching the speedometer hit sixty, seventy, and finally into the clear.

Several anxious miles rolled by before Erik reached for the folding map. Next stop: March Air Force Base.

CHAPTER 40

Red sky in the morning

The dragon swished its tail outside the gates of Babylon. Vengeance was his, or so it appeared.

After fighting the traffic for nearly three hours, the battered Hummer reached the city of Riverside. Waves of citrus glowed against the horizon.

Erik steered through an obstacle course of stalled cars before turning onto Interstate 215 for the last leg of the trip. He glanced affectionately at Heather, fast asleep with her knees against her chest and her head bobbing gently with the rhythm of the road.

Near the intersection of the 91 Freeway and the interstate, the wind gusted through a venturi created by the surrounding hills. Heather screamed, instantly awake.

Erik swerved to miss a jack-knifed big rig. Glancing into the rearview mirror, he watched the roadway ignite in a shower of sparks as the tractor-trailer rig toppled helplessly onto its side. "Did you see that?"

"Who do you think warned you?" she said.

Outside, the sound of car horns and the whoosh of rain.

"Maybe we should go back there, see if we can help."

No sooner had the words left his lips than a highway patrol car flew past them in the opposite direction with its red and blue lights flashing.

Heather stared out the rear window. "There's nothing we

can do, best to let the police handle it."

"Sixty miles inland, and the storm's still dangerous." Erik shook his head. "After you drop me, I want you to head for the Nevada state line."

"What? You can't ditch me out here, I'm staying with you."

"We'll see about that," he said, turning his attention back to the road.

Without warning, a torrent of muddy water surged across the roadway. It slopped over the fenders and buried the windshield. Erik squinted to see. He fumbled with the controls until Heather found the wiper switch and turned it up a notch.

"What would you do without me?" she asked.

"We do make a pretty good team," he admitted, toying with the radio.

A long tone preceded a Civil Defense message from the National Weather Service in San Diego. The report warned of flash flooding.

"Still think it's safe for a woman to drive through the desert alone?"

"We'll talk about it," he said, wondering if he'd missed the base.

Heather pointed with her finger. "There!"

Erik took the turn at fifty-plus and skidded to a stop beside a guard gate. Except for the narrow band of sunlight warming the eastern ridge of mountains, the sky appeared dark and inhospitable. Heavy rain had been falling all night, and muddy runoff filled the ditches bordering the road.

A guard in a raincoat leaned from the protection of his station and motioned for Erik to lower his window.

"Can I help you?" he said.

"I'm with the Department of Weather, at least I used to be with the Department of Weather. Anyway, when the hurricane made landfall we..."

The guard stared at him, unimpressed. As Erik fumbled for his wallet in a desperate search for credentials, Heather leaned across the front seat with her press pass. "I'm a reporter."

"Yes, ma'am," said the guard, with a tip of his cap. "Where you headed?"

"We're looking for the Hurricane Hunters of the 53rd Weather Recon Wing. We'd appreciate it if you would show us the way."

"Sure thing," he said, tearing a map from his clipboard.

Erik couldn't believe it. In less time than it took him to remove his wallet, Heather had the guard eating out of her hand.

The gate went up, and the mud-spattered Hummer slipped inside the base.

"Like fixing a speeding ticket," she said, primping in the visor's lighted mirror.

"Suppose you've done that, too?" he said, winding the Hummer through the base.

"So, what's the plan?" she said. "You do have a plan, don't you? We spent the last three hours risking our lives to get here."

"Of course I have a plan."

"Let's have it?"

"After you drop me, I want you to head east for Las Vegas."

"No way! You wouldn't even be here if not for me. We're partners."

"Look, this might be a one-way ticket, and you're not going, so forget it."

"What are you up to?"

"If I can get to the squadron's commander, I might be able to convince him to attempt an airborne rescue."

Before he could utter another word, the left front tire buried itself a rut. The Hummer shook and the wheel spun in his hands. He steered back onto level pavement and headed for a staging area where several Hercules aircraft waited in formation.

"Think you can find your way back to the guard gate?"

"My daughter's in Florida with her grandparents, my insurance is paid up and I'm on the brink of one of the hottest stories ever. If you think I'm heading back now, Mister, you're sadly mistaken."

The negotiations were getting him nowhere. Besides, she did have a point—if she hadn't freed him from his dockside prison, he would have left Harbor Island in a zippered bag. Any rescue plan would likely include Heather, and Erik knew it.

"Suit yourself."

Chapter 41

Duty calls

Erik parked beside a building overlooking the planes. "This must be the place."

Heather followed him toward the entrance, holding her coat over her head to keep off the rain. She peered through a window in the door, letting her cheek brush against his.

Inside, two flight-suited officers were talking to Deevers.

"What the hell is he doing here?" Erik said.

"Who?"

"Deevers...the guy who fired me, remember?"

"You have to face him sometime."

"You're right," he said, squaring his shoulders and leading her through the door.

"Well, well," Deevers said, "if it isn't Chicken Little and Deep Throat."

"Screw off," said Erik.

"You look like you've been out wrestling pigs."

Erik turned his back on Deevers and approached one of the Air Force officers, a medium-built man with short red hair. The officer studied Erik and rolled a pencil back and forth between the fingers of his left hand.

"I'm Colonel York," the officer said."

"Reynard," Erik said, extending his hand. "And this is Heather Conroy, with Ocean Broadcasting."

"I'd introduce you to Max Deevers, but it appears you

already know each other."

"Unfortunately," said Erik.

Deevers closed the gap between them. "Erik used to be one of my hurricane specialists."

"Your top specialist, remember?"

York motioned to the officer at his side. "This is Lieutenant Colonel Garcia, my copilot."

A low harmonic groan resonated through the building. A moment later, the lights dimmed and the windows shuddered in their frames. Heather leaned into Erik.

"How'd you know we'd be here?" Deevers said.

Erik stepped toward a cluster of weather charts taped to the wall. "I've got a friend at one of our local field offices. He tipped me off, told me the Hurricane Hunters were on their way to March."

Deevers' expression gave him away. "We've got a slight problem."

"That's an understatement."

"Two of your associates are stuck out on Catalina Island, directly in the hurricane's path." Deevers moved toward a weather chart and put his finger on the spot. "Right about here. Problem is, there's no way short of a direct order from Ocean to authorize a rescue."

"I'd like a word with him myself," Erik said.

"Don't hold your breath. He flew out of John Wayne Airport ahead of the storm, and we haven't been able to reach him."

Erik shook his head. The sonofabitch was probably busy counting his illicit gains en route to the Caribbean.

"Even if we could swing a rescue, I'm afraid we'd only put more people at risk," Deevers said. "Tremulous seas and high winds have kept Coast Guard helicopters pinned down and the cutters at port."

Lieutenant Colonel Garcia picked up the first of two ringing phone lines. After putting the first call on hold, he picked up the second line.

"The governor's office is holding on one, FEMA's on two," he said, handing the phone to Deevers. "L.A.'s reporting the worst flooding since '82."

Deevers lifted the receiver and buried himself in the call.

Erik turned to York. "There might be another way. All we have to do is punch through the hurricane and spiral down inside the eye. When the center of the eye passes over the runway, we land, grab our people and get the hell out of there before the backside of the eye catches up with us."

York stared at him. "You realize what you're asking me to do? I've already lost one crew to this storm, I'll be damned if I'll sacrifice another."

"If we don't go in, they don't stand a chance," Erik said. "We can't just leave them out there."

York stared out the window for several long seconds. "You actually think a rescue's possible?"

"Theoretically, yes." Erik cleared a nearby table. "First, the tower needs to patch us through to NASA. They've probably got ER-2s working above the storm. We'll also need access to the Interactive Processing System, all the GOES-10 satellite imagery we can lay our hands on and real-time photo recon of the storm."

Deevers finished his call and lowered the receiver. "Look, nobody wants them out of there more than I do, but this sounds way too risky. The eye last measured ten miles across and shrinking, could be even tighter by the time it passes over the runway."

"So that's it?" Erik said. "We just leave them out there?"

"I'm afraid this mission was doomed before it got off the ground," Deevers said.

York turned slowly from the window with a crazy smile on his face. "I'm not accustomed to leaving good people behind to die. I command this squadron, and with all due respect I don't need your authorization. This just became a military rescue."

Deevers said, "Even if you manage to live through this stunt, you may end up at Elmendorf, de-icing planes for the rest of your career."

"That's a risk I'm willing to take, but I insist on two things. First, I fly the plane. Second, this is strictly a volunteer mission."

"That's easy," Erik said. "I'm going."

No sooner had he volunteered than he felt Heather's hand in his. "Me, too," she said. "After all, the press has the right to document a rescue mission like this firsthand."

"What the hell," Deevers said. "I'm in, but first I've got to get something for my stomach, this acid reflux is killing me."

Erik smiled. Deevers had a conscience after all.

"I've been flying into hurricanes most of my life," York said, leveling his eyes on Erik, "but this is a pretty tall order. You think you can coordinate a landing on that island?"

"Yessir, I do."

"Ever seen the airport?"

"Once."

"And you actually think we can get one of our planes in there?"

"It'll be close, United flew DC-3s in there until 1954. You get me real-time satellite recon of this storm, and I'll thread the needle."

"What about the runway?"

"It's thirty-two-hundred feet long and seventy-five feet wide. Sits atop a hill with a cliff at each end."

"Sounds delightful. Tell me, do you remember everything with that kind of detail?"

"The kid's eidetic," Deevers said, "has a photographic memory."

"So why'd you fire me?"

"That'll be enough," York said, getting between them. "Now, let me get this straight. All we have to do is plow through the worst hurricane on record to get there?" He turned to Deevers. "What do you hear from your people?"

"They're getting pounded pretty hard, made the decision last night to abandon the casino building. The storm's threatening to wash the whole damn thing into the sea."

"Do you think they stand a better chance out in the open?"

"Depends on the storm," Deevers said, fiddling with a nearby radio. "Storm tide's the biggest problem. Last we heard, they'd commandeered a jeep and were holed up at the botanical gardens."

Erik consulted an island map. "That would put them right about here. Flash flooding will likely take out the canyons. Their best bet's to catch Divide Road. From there, they can work their way over to Airport Road and up to the terminal."

"What's so special about the terminal building?"

"It's adjacent to the runway and constructed of concrete-reinforced blocks. It might just hold together long enough for us to get them out of there."

"Who are we risking our necks for anyway?" York asked.

"Two of my people," Deevers said, "Tai Jeffers and..."

"Jeffers?" York interrupted. "Michael Simms' fiancée is out there?"

"That's right."

"Good man, Simms," York lamented. "He and his crew will be sorely missed."

"The other's a visiting professor from Texas Tech, a fellow named Yoshida."

The pencil between York's fingers snapped, and the two halves fell to the floor. Pulling on his cap, he moved toward the door and stared outside at the rain. "I'll be out in the hangar, see if I can round up some JATO bottles."

The door slammed shut behind him, and the room fell silent.

Chapter 42

One way ticket

The copilot straightened his cap and joined Erik and Heather at the window. "York lost his father over Japan during the war, and never had a chance to get to know him."

They stood for a few moments in silence. The copilot zipped up his jacket and motioned down the hall with his chin. "I suggest you grab a couple of flight suits and get out of those wet clothes. It gets pretty cold up there. I'll be outside with York," he added, pausing near the door. "Meet us aboard the plane once you've had a look at those charts."

The storm surge washed several blocks inland, reducing Avalon to little more than a war zone. The pier had vanished beneath the waves, trees were toppled and the last flicker of power had long since gone out.

Boats that had mistakenly sought refuge from the storm by sailing into normally calm Avalon Harbor were beached by the dozen and stacked like driftwood along the shore.

Tai and Yoshida managed to secure the Jeep behind the entrance to the botanical gardens, away from the leading edge of the storm. The wind had blown hard all night, and they'd barely made it that far.

After helping Yoshida lug a short-wave radio inside, Tai tried various frequencies until the Coast Guard picked up the transmission and patched her through to Deevers.

"You have to get us out of here," she begged. "Find some way to get us off this island."

"We're working on it, but you've got to keep your wits about you. Hold on, someone wants to speak with you."

"Tai?"

"Is that you, Erik?"

"Don't worry," he said. "We're gonna get you out of there."

"They should have listened to you," she said. "We all should have listened to you."

"It's all right, everything's going to be okay."

"Do you have any idea what we're going through?"

"Must be scary as hell."

"Damn right," she said.

Yoshida moved to her side.

"We're blind out here," she whimpered. "The weather fax quit the moment we lost our cell service. Where's the eye?"

"It's close, under twenty miles."

"We haven't seen the worst of it?"

"I'm afraid not," he said. "I've got more news...good and bad."

"Give me the good news first—something, anything."

"We're going to land at the airport and fly the two of you out of there."

"You can't land, the wind's screaming."

"That leads me to the bad news," he said. "The hurricane's undergone an explosive deepening."

"How strong?"

"It may not be the largest storm on record, but it's one of the most intense. Winds are topping two hundred."

The microphone fell from Tai's hand as she turned from the radio. She backed against the wall and slid downward until she hit the floor. Yoshida leaned down to retrieve the mike.

"Tai, are you there?"

"No, Erik, it's me...Yoshida."

"Listen, as soon as the eye passes overhead, you need to

head for the airport. Do you copy? Hunker down in the terminal building till we get there, and watch out for flooding in the canyons."

"What if we don't make it?"

"You'll be on your own."

The line crackled with static, and the connection faded in the thin air of silence.

⊚

Back at the base, Erik tried the radio without success.

"Forget it," Deevers said. "They're gone."

Erik shook his head. "Get him, the voice of optimism."

"Volunteered for this mission, didn't I?"

"Come on," Heather said, pulling Erik by the arm. "Let's get suited up."

⊚

A short time later, Heather crossed the room and leaned against the windowsill. Outside, the weather worsened. Erik tucked the latest satellite recon and weather faxes inside his coat and joined her at the window. It was time.

They pushed open the door to the roar of turboprops and sloshed across the tarmac. A single WC-130 Hercules glistened up ahead, its running lights reflecting in the pavement. The intense wind made it difficult to stand, and a man wearing a head-set and parka circled the plane removing wheel blocks. The rain let up momentarily, and Erik led Heather toward the open door.

"What are those?" she hollered, pointing toward the belly of the plane.

Above the wheels were clusters of canisters, four on each side of the aircraft. They looked to measure a little under a foot in diameter and just under a yard long.

"JATO bottles," he said, helping her aboard, "jet assisted takeoff. We used them in the Antarctic when we needed extra thrust."

"Thrust?"

"Relax," he said. "I doubt if we'll need them."

CHAPTER 43

Into the maelstrom

The Lockheed WC-130 taxied toward the end of the runway. Turboprops roared as a bit of morning light reflected against the windshield. Inside, Erik glanced out the side window—visibility was limited, and he hoped they'd be able to find the runway through the rain.

He turned toward Heather and helped her adjust her seat belt. "It's not too late to change your mind."

"And let you boys have all the fun? Not on your life."

"Suit yourself," he said, tightening his own belt to the point of pain. "By the way, I think khaki green's your color."

"You say the sweetest things."

York released the brakes and the plane rumbled down the long runway. The wings flexed as the plane lumbered into the sky.

Erik felt the power as the Hercules began its turn. Heather took his hand and squeezed, managing a weak smile.

The time it took to punch through the eyewall felt like an eternity, but at last they had done it. A deceptively large moat had formed around the vortex, with bands of feeder clouds spiraling inward. The Hercules circled inside the fair weather of the eye, slowly descending.

The plane remained intact, save for a bent radio chassis that had shaken itself loose. Garcia, the copilot, managed to secure the radio so it wouldn't kill anyone and rejoined York in the cockpit. Erik stared out the window, searching for the airport.

"There!" he said, unbuckling his seat belt and getting to his feet. "Off to the right."

York stared downward. "Damn, we missed it."

It took several minutes for the plane to come around again. Erik made his way to the cockpit and wedged himself between the navigator's seat and the copilot.

"What the hell are you doing up here?" York said, whipping off his headphones. "Get back to your seat."

"As soon as you get a fix on the runway."

The eyewall encircled them like a spinning stadium. They were now at the center of the meteorological machine, the storm's innermost axis.

"Look." Erik pointed. "I can see the runway."

The edge of the eyewall couldn't have been more than two miles off when York began his descent. Time was precious.

York said, "We might just have a shot at it. Now, would you please get back to your seat?"

"Yes, sir."

Beyond the runway, the terminal building and tower came into view. York pushed the nose down, and Erik felt the sudden descent just below his navel. He turned toward Heather—despite her bravado, she was looking pretty green.

"Here you go," he said, handing her a plastic bag.

"What's this?" she groaned.

"It's a burp bag, in case you..."

Before he could finish, Heather had the bag against her mouth and her head between her knees. He gently patted her back, hoping it would help.

"She'll feel better once I get this baby on the ground," York hollered. "Best to let her get some fresh air before we get airborne again."

"Roger," Erik replied.

Heather let out a long moan as the plane sailed toward the tower.

Erik studied the passing landscape. When he failed to spot his friends beside the runway, he felt his stomach drop.

York glanced at Erik. "I hope you know what you're doing. According to the tower back at March, the storm's on the move."

"Don't worry about me," Erik said. "Just keep flying the airplane."

"Once I put this bird on the ground, you've got ten minutes, tops. Your people better be there with their bags packed."

"They'll be there."

Phenomenal seas pounded the island's rugged shoreline. Beyond a rocky cliff were the runway, tower and terminal buildings. No jeep, no Tai, no Yoshida.

The plane continued its descent, and Erik studied the terminal building's roof. Most of the clay tiles were gone, but the walls were still standing. Beyond the airport he could see the approaching eyewall.

A pocket of turbulence rattled the plane, and Erik spun toward Deevers. "Enjoying the ride?"

"Two years until I retire, and he wants to know if I'm enjoying the damn ride."

Sparring with Deevers took Erik's mind off the risky business at hand. So far, he'd done his part, threading the needle as promised.

Heather knotted the burp bag and sat upright. She gave Erik a weak smile and slid a piece of gum between her lips.

York stared at the encroaching eyewall. "I'm getting squeezed here, looks like she's spinning up."

"What's he talking about?" Heather asked.

"The winds in the eyewall are accelerating, like an ice skater drawing in her arms. The smaller the eye, the faster the rotation."

"This mission was marginal to begin with," York grumbled. "We're gonna need every inch of runway to get off the ground."

Erik tapped Deevers on the arm. "Have they heard from Bobby Ocean?"

"Not a word."

The plane came in steep and hot, gaining speed on its descent. Erik heard little above the growl of the Allison turboprops, and he yawned to equalize the pressure.

Heather gripped his arm as the landing gear locked into place. "If we make it, how would you like to pick up where we left off?"

Erik smiled. "Sounds like you're asking me out."

"Hold on," York interrupted.

Outside the window, the ground came up fast. Light funneled in from above, and the runway raced into view. Despite York's experienced touch, the plane rolled unsteadily from side to side.

"Easy, Red," the copilot warned. "Grease it on, boy, just a few more feet."

The wheels smoked against the runway, and the engines roared. The WC-130 bucked when the paving failed to fully support its weight, leaving a rutted runway in its trail.

The plane shook uncontrollably.

"I thought you said the runway would hold," York hollered.

"I said it could handle a DC-3 and gave you the dimensions," Erik said. "It's a little late now."

"Feels like slurry," York said. "Lucky we're still in one piece."

Suddenly, a chunk from one of the tires pitched upward, into the underside of the wing. Halfway down the runway, the Hercules eased out of the ruts as the surface began to hold.

"Where in the hell are your people?" York said. "We don't have all day."

"I think I saw something," Erik called from the doorway. "How do you get this door open?"

"Let me bring us to a stop first, damn it!"

In a matter of seconds, Garcia was at his side, working at the door. Erik ran in place, like a marathoner warming up.

Deevers glanced toward the door. "Hey, Erik?"

"Yeah."

"Watch yourself out there, okay?"

Erik smiled. "I never knew you cared."

Heather rose unsteadily to her feet. "I'm coming with you."

"Don't even think about it, you're needed here on the plane."

She stared at Erik for a moment, then slid back into her seat.

"Remember," York said, "ten minutes. If you're not back, we're out of here."

CHAPTER 44

Race against the wind

Erik hit the pavement running. The water sheeted across the runway, drenching him to the knees. He listened to the sound of his own breathing and watched the Hercules begin its slow turn.

A half-mile out he stopped to scan the horizon and called out to his friends, then back into cadence, his knees pumping. Off in the distance, the eyewall continued its implacable advance.

Beyond the terminal building and halfway down a paved road, two small figures slowly advanced. Tai raised her arms in a panicked salute, trying to flag him down. Erik changed course and picked up speed. He could see them more clearly now, exhausted and wet. Tai wrapped her arm around Yoshida, urging him ahead. He appeared to be injured.

"Come on," Erik hollered as the plane completed its turn. "We don't have much time."

Yoshida hobbled up the road, favoring his good leg. "I think it's sprained."

Erik wrapped his arm around Yoshida's back and helped him along. The better part of ten minutes had elapsed by the time they finally reached the crest of the hill.

Across the tarmac, the Hercules spooled its engines, preparing for its one-way sprint down the runway. Tai broke into a full run. She waved her arms in the direction of the plane while Erik and Yoshida plodded ahead.

York must have seen them, because the plane suddenly shut

down—abandoning its takeoff roll. The storm was on the move, and the eyewall was closing in fast.

Erik bore most of Yoshida's weight, nearly running by the time he reached the runway. Tai raced toward the plane.

Inside the cockpit, York unbuckled his harness and turned to his copilot. "Take over."

The propellers were a blur, and the door sprang open. Deevers stood in the opening, beckoning with his arm.

"Come on," he yelled. "Hurry!"

Erik heard a crash and glanced over his shoulder. Less than a mile away, a utility building exploded into a thousand pieces.

York joined Deevers in the open doorway. Tai reached the plane first and hurled herself inside. Erik and the old man were next. Reaching from the open doorway, York gripped Yoshida by the arm.

Erik bounded aboard a moment later, and the plane began moving before the door had fully closed. York belted Yoshida into the navigator's seat, then fastened his own harness.

"Easy, now," said the copilot. "Watch those ruts."

Heather held onto Erik like she'd never let him go. Outside, the too-short runway sailed past. If they didn't get their speed up, they'd topple from the cliff at the end of the runway and disappear beneath the waves.

Beads of sweat glistened on Deevers forehead. "Can't you taxi to the end of the runway and get a full run at it?"

"No time for that," York said. "The eyewall's nearly on top of us."

Erik stared out the window. He was right, it was nearly on top of them.

The Hercules rumbled down the runway.

"Damn it!" York hollered. "There's a problem with the flaps. We must have damaged the hydraulics."

Deevers wiped the sweat from his forehead and cinched his seat belt. Across the plane, Tai closed her eyes and bit her thumbnail. They were past the point of no return.

Erik watched the end of the runway race into view, the cliff beyond. He gazed over at Heather. If these were to be his last few moments, he was glad to be spending them with her.

"We'll never make it," warned the copilot.

"That's it," said York. "Light the bottles."

The plane shimmied as the runway began to give. Garcia engaged the JATO bottles, and all eight rockets deployed. Erik felt the sudden thrust as the Hercules went ballistic.

Just then, a herd of bison stampeded toward the runway. The nose gear began to rise, but the rear wheels were still down. There was no turning back, no killing the JATOs. York drew back on the yoke.

The herd hit the edge of the runway and scattered. The plane bore down on them, wheels barely inching off the ground.

York struggled with the controls. "Climb, you sonofabitch!"

The animals fanned out in front of them, and Erik drew Heather close. Miraculously, York managed to miss the herd. A moment later the plane sailed clear of the runway and dipped, the fuselage coming perilously close to the wave tops. York banked the Hercules inside the radius of the eye, and the plane began its lazy helix toward the sun.

Erik peered toward the cockpit. York was talking to Yoshida, smiling intermittently, making exaggerated gestures as if pantomiming the details of their narrow escape. Two old warriors making peace.

Deevers was back on the radio, speaking excitedly to someone at the National Hurricane Center.

When they reached an altitude of ten thousand feet, the Hercules leveled off and sailed toward the eyewall, the deadliest part of the storm.

"Tighten those belts," York hollered.

Deevers glanced nervously about the cabin. "It's gonna get rough."

The plane shuddered as it punched its way back through the clouds. Heather gripped Erik by the arm, staring wide-eyed out the window. Intense rain pelted the glass.

Stressed to the limits of its design, the Hercules groaned. York struggled with the controls, cautiously navigating his way out of the storm.

Deevers listened intently through a radio headset. "I'll be damned, the hurricane changed course. Looks like it's moving out to sea."

Despite the nightmarish conditions outside, Erik felt a somber wave of relief. It would take years for the coast to fully recover, but they'd been spared the sustained fury of the storm, the endless rain and monsoon-like flooding.

Sunlight flashed outside the windows, and the shaking began to subside. Aside from a flock of disoriented birds, they were alone in the sky. They had done it, made it safely through the eyewall.

Erik turned toward Deevers. "Any news on Ocean's whereabouts?"

"His plane went down in the storm," he said, pulling off his headset. "Radar just confirmed it."

"Have they begun a search?"

"The water's too deep for divers, over a thousand feet near the crash site. I'm afraid it's looking more like a salvage job than a rescue mission."

Tai stared blankly out the window, expressionless except for a single tear glistening down her cheek.

Deevers glanced back at Erik. "Looks like your friend Samuelson may have been right. Tell you what, a few things are going to change when I get back to Miami. I promise you that. I've got an empty office if you're interested."

"Maybe, but first I plan on collaborating with an investigative reporter I know."

Heather nuzzled Erik's shoulder. "I'll put in a good word with the network. I can see you now—suit, tie and a fresh carnation in your lapel."

Deevers simply shook his head. "Reynard a TV weatherman? That'll be the day."

EPILOGUE

Several thousand miles away, the trade winds had calmed. A Coast Guard Falcon jet flying drug interdiction screamed across the Caribbean at low altitude, bound for Tobago. Off in the distance, an orange dot bobbed on the horizon. A lone signal flare streaked into the sky, and the Falcon adjusted its course.

Less than a minute later, the jet passed through the vapor trail left by the flare. Beneath them, a welcome sight. What had appeared to be nothing more than a small dot at a distance of three miles, now appeared to be a raft, the type of life raft carried aboard the planes of the 53rd Weather Recon Wing.